AUNT CLAIRE'S
PET CARE

aunt clairE's
SECrEt

Katie Evans

KATIE EVANS

Edited by Twyla Beth Lambert

Cover design by Fresh Design

Cover art by Tincho Schmidt

Print ISBN 978-1-957529-07-3

Ebook ISBN 978-1-957529-08-0

LCCN 2023939052

For Tyler. It's all for you, Tyler.

ONE

Isabel was covered in soap, water, and dog hair. And she was furious.

"Hold him still!" Maya shouted, pushing a wet strand of hair off her face.

"No. You hold him. I'll wash him. He likes me better, and you're stronger." Isabel struggled to stay standing as Freddy jumped up on her with his front paws.

The yard behind the veterinary clinic was mostly used for exercise for the animals, but Aunt Claire had a bath built in the far corner. The animals always wanted to play back there so the sisters had a hard time with this chore.

Freddie shook hard, spraying the girls with water, suds, and wet-dog smell. He wagged his tail and stared at the girls with his mouth open and his tongue out. One of his ears stood up, and the other laid down. Isabel found him quite cute. It was her sister that was so irritating.

Maya stood up tall, towering over Isabel. Stomping her foot in a puddle, she splashed water all over Isabel. Isabel turned the hose and shot water at Maya in revenge.

"You are so annoying! Why do you have to make everything difficult? Grow up!"

"Me? You're supposed to be some amazing, all-star athlete, and you can't even hold this little dog still."

Freddie saw his chance. He jumped from the bath and ran into the yard, leaving a trail of soap in the grass as he went. He found a dirt spot, laid down, and began rolling around joyfully.

Maya screamed in frustration just as Aunt Claire came out of the side door that led to her off-limits laboratory.

"Geez! What's going on out here?"

Maya and Isabel started talking over each other, blaming the other for the bath-time disaster.

Aunt Claire sighed. She called to Freddie, and he obediently trotted over. She told him to sit and stay. He did.

"No fair," Isabel whined. "You're the animal whisperer."

Aunt Claire laughed. "I've been a vet for 20 years, Izzie. I've picked up a few things along the way."

Aunt Claire stayed to help the girls finish Freddie's bath.

"You girls need to learn to work together," Aunt Claire said. "Having a sister is a gift. I miss mine every day."

She gave the girls a small, sad smile before walking back through the lab door. The girls avoided looking at each other. The guilt and grief were too heavy.

"Do you ever wonder what's in there?" Isabel asked Maya as they walked back inside the animal clinic.

"Research and stuff, I guess," Maya answered. "Probably, like chemicals she doesn't want us near."

Isabel stared at the lab door.

"Don't go in there," Maya warned. She might have been the older sister, but sometimes she sounded just like a mom.

"It's the only thing she asks us not to do. After everything she's done for us since Mom and Dad died, the least we can do is stay out of her lab."

They walked into the clinic and were greeted by cats, dogs, and birds. Aunt Claire was a well-respected animal expert. People even brought her wild animals in need of assistance or exotic pets that no one else could help. Isabel's favorite was a hawk that Aunt Claire had nursed back to health, who repaid them all by dropping dead rodents in their laps when they least expected it. They'd named him Nolan, and he squawked at them as they walked by.

It wasn't the life Isabel pictured herself having a year ago, before the accident, but she was grateful for it. After Mom and Dad died, Aunt Claire had not hesitated to take the girls in. She even bought a bigger house to make them more comfortable. She provided all the love and support she could and helped with everything from homework to breaking up arguments.

Maya was right. The least they could do was stay out of her lab.

THE NEXT DAY, Isabel typed furiously on her keyboard in computer programming class. Her brown eyes narrowed as she stared at the screen. Mr. Marcks looked at her suspiciously through his thick glasses. He had only asked them to input a simple line of code, but Isabel's computer programming skills far exceeded the others', and she tended to run with her own projects. She'd gotten into programming early in elementary school and was a decent hacker by fifth grade. A girl named Tavi looked at her in awe, and Isabel almost managed to smile at her.

She sat in the back corner of the middle school computer lab with her screen facing into the walls and her books piled on the only side where Mr. Marcks might be able to glance at her screen. No one sat near her. She preferred it that way.

I can't believe how simple the school's security system is, Isabel thought. She had already gotten past all the security features and was curiously poking around the school's file network. Not for any particular reason, but just to see if she could. She could access almost anything just by breaking through the school's basic security features. Everything was so simple here in Horton.

Before Mom and Dad died, she and Maya lived in sunny Anaheim, California. There were traffic jams and tech companies. While technically still in California, Horton couldn't have been more different. There was only one middle school and one high school, and they were right next to each other. Instead of tech companies and office buildings, there were feed stores and hiking shops. And instead of sitting in traffic, they drove on two-lane roads that curved through the foothills of the Sierras. Isabel didn't mind the change. The landscape was beautiful with mountain views. She liked the big oak trees and the sounds of owls hooting instead of horns honking. She even had to watch out for poison oak, which made her feel a little adventurous. Maybe the best part was that she got to know all the animals who came to Aunt Claire's clinic. Plus, she still had a pretty decent internet connection.

Isabel was different now, too. Before the accident, Isabel had been outgoing and friendly. She'd had a lot of friends at her old school, but now she preferred the solitude of her screen. She found it easier to get lost in the world of programming code than to talk to people about herself and her life.

Mr. Marcks told the class to wrap up their work.

"I hope to see you all at the big volleyball game at the high school tonight. Isabel, I'm sure your sister will make us all proud, as usual."

Isabel scoffed. Maya's big game was the last thing that would make her *proud.*

She packed up her things and left the room. She walked into the parking lot to find Maya standing next to her little blue car. She'd saved up every penny she could to buy it after getting her license last month. She was so happy about it that she almost didn't mind having to pick Isabel up every day after school. Maya stood with her arms across her chest, looking up and nodding hopefully. A piece of her wild, long dark hair fell in front of her face, and she tucked it behind her ear. Isabel walked closer to see who she was talking to.

No wonder she's so nervous, she thought as she spotted Andrew talking to Maya.

Andrew was the captain of the water polo team at the high school. He was tall and handsome, and he had one big dimple when he smiled. He was always really nice... even to little sisters. Isabel figured he was there to pick up his own little sister, Sara.

"Hey Izzie," said Andrew with a warm smile. "Good talking to you, Maya. Good luck tonight."

"Will you be there?" Maya asked, her voice slightly higher pitched than normal.

"Of course. Everyone will be."

Maya and Isabel got into their car.

"Oh Andrew, you're so dreamy," mocked Isabel.

"Shut up."

"You have a crush on him."

"You're such a child. I don't have crushes anymore."

Isabel laughed at Maya.

"Sor-*ry*, Miss-Super-Cool-High-School-Student. I didn't realize you were so mature and sophisticated."

Maya clenched her teeth. Her face reddened.

"You're such a brat. Can't you just mind your own business?"

"'Cause you're so good at that?"

"I'm better than you are. Maybe if you would have minded your own business last year when Mom and Dad were still around, they wouldn't have had to go to that stupid school meeting!"

Isabel gasped. She could not believe that Maya was blaming her... even though she sometimes blamed herself. Their parents were killed in a car crash on the way to an after-school meeting after Isabel had caused some trouble nosing around in the district's system.

"Are you saying it's my fault?"

Maya didn't answer.

Isabel felt sick. She had blamed herself before, but she never thought Maya did. Maya stared straight ahead; her jaw clenched. Her knuckles turned white as she squeezed the steering wheel.

When they got home, Aunt Claire greeted them, but both girls stomped to their bedrooms, slamming their doors in a crash that shook the house. In the living room, the two bright white cockatoos with yellow crowns shouted, "TROUBLE! TROUBLE! TROUBLE!"

Isabel threw herself onto her bed and covered her face. A few minutes later, Aunt Claire quietly came in.

"Izzie, are you okay?"

Isabel sat up. Tears streamed down her cheeks.

"I hate Maya," she whispered, her voice cracking.

"Aw, sweetie, you don't hate her. You're sisters. Sisters fight sometimes, especially 11 and 16-year-old sisters."

"She said it's my fault Mom and Dad are dead."

Aunt Claire's mouth dropped open, and her eyes widened. She ran her fingers through her sleek, dark hair and exhaled.

"It is not your fault. And if Maya said that, she is wrong, and I'm sure she didn't mean it. I'll talk to her."

"It doesn't matter," Isabel replied. "She can say whatever she wants. I don't care what she says about me because she's a jerk."

"Izzie, I know what Maya said was terrible, but you two are sisters. You're going to be sisters forever. You are so lucky to have each other."

It was always hard to talk like this with Aunt Claire. She and Mom had been best friends. She would never understand what it was like to have a rotten sister like Maya.

Isabel remembered when she was little, and Mom and Aunt Claire would take her and Maya to the pool together. They would lay in lounge chairs, talking and laughing all day. Their naturally bronzed skin shimmered in the sun, and their wide smiles were contagious. She could never imagine spending a day like that with Maya.

After Aunt Claire left, Isabel stomped all around her room. She couldn't sit down or be still. She couldn't focus. Her skin flushed red, and her hands were balled into fists. Then she had an idea. She slipped her laptop into her backpack and walked into the living room, ready to go to Maya's big game.

MAYA KEPT TAKING BIG, deep breaths. She was dressed in her volleyball uniform with the tiny shorts and the knee pads. She had her hair pulled back into a tight braid that hung halfway down her back. She kept stretching in the car.

"You're going to be great," Aunt Claire told her. "Just think, this time next week we could be driving to the playoffs."

Maya pressed her lips together and nodded.

"Isn't it great, Izzie?" Aunt Claire tried to get her excited.

"Yeah. Great."

As they arrived at the school, Aunt Claire's cell phone rang.

"Go ahead girls, I'll catch up."

Maya and Isabel walked as far apart from each other as they could toward the school, but before they arrived, Aunt Claire shouted to them. She jogged to catch up.

"Maya, I am so sorry, but there is an emergency at the zoo. They need an extra pair of hands urgently. I wouldn't miss your game unless it was a real emergency."

"I know, Aunt Claire. It's okay, really."

She handed Maya the car keys.

"Dr. Franklin is going to pick me up here, and we'll drive to the zoo together." She gave her a squeeze. "I know you'll be great. Please call me after the game. Izzie, take some pictures, okay?"

Isabel smiled. This would make her plan even easier.

Maya and Isabel looked at each other before storming off in separate directions. As Maya headed to the locker room, Isabel walked toward the audio/visual closet that housed the hardware for the school's servers. She looked around to make sure no one was watching before she slipped inside and closed the door behind her. She pulled her laptop out and connected herself to the network.

This is just too easy, she thought.

The high school gym was full of people. Most wore purple and gold, the school colors. Digital monitors that usually showed the cafeteria menu and school announcements had been changed to an animation that said, "Go Knights!" One person even had his face painted. Maya and her team stepped out onto the clean, shiny court, prompting a cheer from the crowd.

If they won this game, they would go to the playoffs and have a chance at winning the state championship. Isabel knew the pressure was on for the whole team.

Isabel sat as far up the bleachers as she could, tucked into a corner at the top.

The energy was intense, and it seemed like everyone was there. Isabel spotted some of her own teachers from the middle school and plenty of her classmates. Andrew was there, sitting with the water polo team. Isabel almost felt guilty for what she was about to do. Almost.

Isabel waited for Maya's big moment. It didn't take long. Early in the first match, Maya leapt into the air and spiked the ball across the net. The other team missed it, and Maya's team got a point. Everyone cheered. Maya high-fived her teammates. Isabel pushed a key on her keyboard.

A second later, people began to laugh quietly, and a few pointed to the monitors. More and more people looked up and began to laugh. Eventually it got Maya's attention.

Gone was the "Go Knights" animation and in its place was a photo of Maya. It was from a day she wasn't feeling well and had just woken up. Her hair looked like a rat's nest, and her eyes and nose were red. Caught off guard when Isabel had taken it, her mouth was hanging open and she had one eye closed. She was wearing an old pajama shirt with emoji faces on it.

Maya's eyes went wide, then her face dropped into a frown. She turned away from it. She quickly began to look around, her face reddening and lips pursed together. Isabel ducked behind a big man sitting on the bleachers watching the game, but Maya spotted her. For a second, Isabel thought Maya might run off the court and attack her, but Maya just stared at Isabel, then swung her braid behind her, pulled her shoulders back, and returned to her position on the court.

Meanwhile, the coach and school principal were yelling for someone to take the photo down. No one at the game seemed to know how.

Maya interrupted them. "It's fine. Let's play."

"We will fix this, Maya," the coach told her, patting her shoulder.

"Really, I don't mind. Let's just get back to the game."

The principal sighed.

"I'll turn off the monitors," he said. "Get back to the game. Go Knights!"

The team played hard and strategically. The Knights won the first match, but the other team won the second.

The final match was tense. Except for ball hits and squeaky shoes, the gym was quiet between points, then boomed with sound each time the Knights scored. They had 14 points—just one more would be a win for them.

Isabel sat back in the bleachers with her arms crossed. She was satisfied that she had gotten Maya back, even if Maya was too cool to show it.

The ball volleyed back and forth over the net four times. It was coming back to the Knights and was headed toward the edge of the court when Maya came out of nowhere. She jumped high into the air and spiked the ball back at the other team. It caught them completely off guard. One girl made a dive and almost got there, but she was too slow. The ball spiked off the court. The Knights won.

The crowd leapt to their feet, screaming and cheering. A chant began, "Ma-ya! Ma-ya! Ma-ya!" The teammates drew in for a big group hug, and everyone high-fived Maya, including the coach.

It took a long time for Maya to come out to the car. Her wide smile disappeared when she saw Isabel. Maya pushed the unlock button on the key fob, and Isabel quickly climbed into the back seat and shut the door. Maya waved cheerfully at a few of her teammates who were gathered nearby. She slipped into the driver's seat silently, without looking at Isabel.

Isabel's phone chimed. She pulled it from her backpack and saw a message from Aunt Claire.

"Aunt Claire asked if we could go to the clinic and get some of her supplies," said Isabel. She'd also asked how the game went, but Isabel did not want to talk to Maya more than she had to. She didn't answer the text.

At the clinic, Maya fumbled with the locks, pushed the door open, and let it close on Isabel. She turned on the lights, and the girls walked through the lobby to the back area where the supplies and offices were.

Isabel accidentally bumped into Maya. That finally set her off.

"What is wrong with you?" Maya hissed at her. "Why would you do that to me?"

"Because you deserved it."

All the dogs in the clinic kennels started barking.

"Deserved it?"

"Yes! You told me it's my fault Mom and Dad died!"

"You are selfish and childish. You were then, and you are now."

With that, Maya stormed into the back room. Nolan, the hawk, squawked loudly at them. Isabel followed her, slamming the door behind her. Isabel stomped around the clinic.

"You think because you're some cool athlete that you have never done anything wrong. You have. You aren't perfect, Maya, so stop acting like you are."

Maya turned and threw the keys at Isabel. Isabel ducked, and the keys hit the ground, sliding under the door to the research lab.

The girls stopped dead in their tracks. They both stared at the door.

"What do we do now?" Isabel asked.

Maya walked over to the door then laid down on the floor, looking under the crack.

"I can't see the keys. They must have slid back there. We have to go in, I guess."

Isabel knew she shouldn't be, but she was excited. She had always wanted to know what was going on in the lab, and while she wanted to obey Aunt Claire's instruction, they had a good reason now. She had butterflies in her stomach.

"We have to get them," said Isabel. "Aunt Claire keeps the keys in the front office, in the top drawer."

Maya silently walked away and came back a moment later with the keys in her hand. Isabel crept closer and closer, looking over Maya's shoulder as she turned the lock. Maya reached for the doorknob and turned it. She pushed the door open slowly, and the girls stepped inside.

TWO

The lab was dark and smelled of sterilizers. Isabel found a light switch and turned it on, holding her breath in anticipation, but the lab looked perfectly normal, with steel tables lined up against one side and a counter with empty beakers lined up on it. Toward the back, a large dry erase board that took up almost a whole wall caught her attention. There were diagrams drawn all over it in different colors—pictures that looked like twisted ladders. Off in the corner sat a desk with a computer and several notebooks. Two very large kennels held a beautiful black Labrador and a small brown goat.

The girls walked around slowly, both pretending to look for the keys while searching for a clue as to what went on in here.

Suddenly a deep voice said, "No."

The girls jumped. Maya slammed against a table.

Isabel looked around for the source of the voice. "Who's there?"

"No," the voice said again.

Maya walked toward the kennels.

"No," said the dog.

Isabel raised her eyebrows as realization hit her. "Can that dog talk?"

"I think it can. Can you talk, little guy?"

"No," the dog said again.

Isabel bent down and pet him. He leaned into her hand and wagged his tail.

"Maybe he can only say *no*," Isabel said.

"I think that's right. But how is that possible?"

"Do you think the goat can talk? Hello, goat, can you talk?"

The goat looked up at Isabel and walked closer to her. She reached her hand inside and scratched him behind the ear.

"Hello? Can you say *no*?"

The goat continued to enjoy the ear scratch silently.

Maya walked closer to the dry erase board and looked carefully at the diagrams.

"I think this is genetics," she said. "We are learning about genetics in my science class right now, and this looks similar. It's like DNA and stuff. It's what gives something their traits. Like black hair or green eyes."

Isabel gasped. "Genetic modification. That's what's going on in here. I read about this online. There are theories that genetics could be changed in some way to allow new characteristics. They do it with plants all over the world. I bet she changed the genetic makeup of this dog so it could talk."

"That's impossible."

"Well obviously, but this dog is talking, isn't it?"

Isabel joined Maya near the diagrams.

"Look, see how she drew the DNA with a different

color here," Isabel pointed. "I bet that's the part she modified."

"Is this legal? Can people do this kind of research?"

"I don't know," said Isabel. "Maybe that's why we aren't allowed in here."

Just then, the door swung open and in walked Aunt Claire.

AUNT CLAIRE and the girls stood staring at each other for a long time before Isabel broke the silence.

"We didn't mean to, Aunt Claire. The keys slid under the door, and we had to get them. We weren't snooping around. Honest. We just—"

"Izzie, Izzie. It's okay," Aunt Claire interrupted. "I'm sure you didn't mean to. You didn't text me back, so I came here myself."

She sighed heavily and glanced all around the room.

"So, you figured out what we're doing here?"

Maya nodded.

"Is genetic modification illegal? Is that why this is a secret?"

Aunt Claire shook her head. "I don't even know where to begin explaining this to you."

Isabel looked at the dog. "Start here. Did you modify this dog so he could talk?"

"Yes and no," Aunt Claire answered. "Our intention here is to create service animals for people with disabilities. My research partners and I attempted to modify Herbert here so that he could speak to his owner, but we haven't advanced that far. We don't ever expect an animal to be able to speak like you and I do, but we hope to be able to get them close to what a parrot could do. If the dog can tell people simple things, like *no*, which I'm sure Herbert said to you, he could prevent a blind person from stepping into traffic or touching a hot stove."

Isabel's mind was blown. She'd always known Aunt Claire was brilliant, but this was incredible.

"What about the goat?" Maya asked.

"Oh, sweet Daisy here is our best success story yet." Aunt Claire opened Daisy's kennel and let her roam out toward the girls. "By adding a specific protein to her DNA, we have altered the makeup of her milk. The milk Daisy produces now has the components to create medications that could save people's lives."

Daisy nudged Isabel's pocket looking for something to chew on.

"She seems like a normal goat," Maya laughed.

"She is. Except she gets pretty special treatment around here." Aunt Claire walked over to a jar on the counter and produced a handful of treats for Daisy, who took them greedily. "She's pretty spoiled."

Aunt Claire stepped toward Herbert, who bounded toward her, and she provided him a treat as well.

"No," he said. Isabel giggled.

"As you can see, we still have some work to do with Herbert. He can say simple, one-syllable words, but he doesn't know what they mean yet. It will require more training and potentially more research to get it right."

"This is amazing," Maya said. "Why didn't you tell us about this before?"

"That's the tricky part," Aunt Claire sighed. "Look, I rushed back because I needed some medications for the zoo. I need to go back there. You two go home, and I promise we can talk more tomorrow."

ISABEL LAID IN BED, thinking of all the possibilities of what she had learned. Freddie, the mud-loving dog from the clinic, was staying with them until a kennel opened back up. He was curled against her. She stroked his soft fur, nice and clean after his bath, as her mind raced. Service animals that could talk! Animals that could produce medicine! Who knows what else! She was overwhelmed with pride for Aunt Claire. Not only was she incredibly smart, but she was doing all this work to try to help people who needed it most.

Unable to sleep, Isabel pulled her laptop onto the bed and began searching for information on this type of science. She was fascinated to learn that genetic research was being done all over the world—plants were being altered to grow in different climates, animals were being used to produce important and necessary materials, and governments all over the world were trying to get a handle on whether they approved of it.

Freddie huffed in annoyance at Isabel's movement. He dug under the covers and burrowed his way into the darkness.

Isabel learned many people are opposed to genetic modification. Some believe it is unsafe. Others say it violates their religious beliefs. Maybe this was why Aunt Claire was keeping her work a secret.

THE NEXT MORNING, Isabel woke up with her computer still open on the bed. She must have dozed off in the middle of her research. Isabel could smell breakfast from down the hall. She slipped out of bed and wandered into the kitchen, her hair sticking up all over and her pajamas wrinkled.

"Good morning," Aunt Claire chimed as she saw her. "I made waffles."

Isabel smiled and poured herself a glass of orange juice.

"So how was the game?"

Isabel grimaced. "Well, I kind of tried to ruin it, but Maya didn't let me, and they won."

"Do I even want to know?"

"Probably not."

Aunt Claire shook her head.

"Maya scored the winning point in the last match. She was really awesome. The crowd was even cheering her name."

"Wow. That's pretty cool."

"Yeah. I bet it's amazing to have people think you're so great."

"Hey. You're pretty great, too."

Isabel shrugged.

"You are. You're brilliant and clever. Your talents might not get showcased like an athlete's, but we both know you have some serious brainpower. It's kind of scary, really."

"It is totally scary," said Maya as she came around the corner.

"Congrats on the big win!" Aunt Claire came around the counter and hugged her.

Maya sat at the table next to Isabel. The sun came shining in through the sliding glass door on the other side of the room. It was going to be a beautiful fall Saturday.

Aunt Claire brought a big plate of waffles to the table and sat down with the girls.

"I have some important stuff I need to tell you," she started. "It's about my research."

The girls leaned forward in their chairs.

"Have you ever heard of genetically modified organisms, or GMOs?"

"Only what I've read on the internet," said Isabel.

"I've heard a little bit about it," Maya added. "But I think you should still just start from the beginning."

"GMO means that someone has changed the genetic makeup of a plant or animal. For example, altering a crop so that it can grow with less water. In my case, I'm trying to merge traits of different animals together."

"How would that work?" Maya asked.

"All living things—even plants—are made up of billions of strands of DNA. DNA is like the blueprint for all our physical characteristics. For example, it determines if you have blue or brown eyes."

"Oh yeah," Maya nodded quickly. "We learned about DNA in school."

Isabel nodded. "The diagrams that look like twisty ladders, right?"

"Right. DNA has millions of pieces of code—like a computer program, Izzie. And those pieces of code determine our traits."

"If you change the code, you change the traits. Just like how, if I change some text in a piece of programming, it changes the output?" Isabel stated.

"So, you mix animals together?" asked Maya.

"Sort of. I'm filling in the gaps of the DNA with code from other animals. The goal is to give them more abilities. For example, I could take the sense of smell from a bloodhound and give it to a hawk..."

"Nolan!" shouted Isabel.

Aunt Claire smiled. "Nolan was one of my first experiments. I did not get the results I was looking for, but he was an important early step in my research. I tell everyone I rescued him, but the truth is that he was part of some research. I just loved him so much I brought him home."

Aunt Claire's smiled disappeared suddenly, and she added, "But GMOs are very controversial, girls. Not everyone agrees that humans should be altering animals like this."

"Is that why you keep your lab a secret?" Isabel asked.

"Not exactly, though that's part of it. I am working on GMOs that could really help people in need. My work is funded by a grant that sees the benefit in this kind of research. So, I'm working in partnership with other scientists to help create service animals. If I could teach a dog to speak, it could perhaps call for help if a disabled person fell. But there are other people out there who see GMOs as a potential for all kinds of different things—like unnaturally strong guard dogs or animals that could be used like weapons. Some researchers see this as a way to make a lot of money. If the information fell into the wrong hands, it could be used for anything."

"We won't tell anyone, Aunt Claire. Don't worry. Maybe we can even help you," Isabel said.

"Hold on, hold on. There's more. There is one researcher in particular. His name is Dr. Steve Rodriguez. We actually collaborated on some projects in the past. Dr. Rodriguez is backed by some big money, but they haven't seen much success yet. He has tried to recruit me to work for him, and I've refused because I know they don't have good intentions. Dr. Rodriguez has no idea how far I have gotten or what kind of success I am having. I try not to underestimate what he would do to get his hands on my research. He's under a lot of pressure to produce results."

"You think he would steal your data?" Maya asked.

"I do. That is why it must be kept secret. I need you two to understand this information getting out could have serious consequences. Not just for me, but for the world. It could seriously change the intent of genetic engineering. Do you understand?"

"Yes," they both said.

Isabel sat quietly eating her waffles after that, but her mind was racing. She knew what she needed to do, and she was creating a plan.

THREE

By the time Monday came around, Isabel was practically an expert on GMOs. She'd spent hours reading everything she could find on the internet about it. From what she'd learned, it was pretty clear Aunt Claire was way ahead of other researchers who had published their work so far. No one had come anywhere near getting a dog to speak, even just one word.

She spent her time in programming class doing the research she would need to carry out her plan. Sometimes she really felt bad for Mr. Marcks, who was always trying to work with her and always shut out. He had tried to ask what she was working on, but she certainly couldn't fill him in.

When it was time to leave, Maya was outside with Andrew again. They were standing closer together now than before.

Someone called her name behind her, and she turned to see Sara.

"What's going on with those two?" Sara asked mischievously.

Isabel shrugged.

"Do you think Maya's into him?"

"Probably. Aren't all the girls into him?"

"Yeah. But I don't know why. He's a total dork."

Isabel chuckled.

"See you later," said Sara, and she headed for their car.

"See ya."

Isabel hadn't made any friends since they had moved here. She wondered, if circumstances were different, if Sara could have been one.

She walked around to the passenger seat of Maya's Honda.

"Don't say anything," Maya said.

"About what?"

"About Andrew. I already know what you're thinking."

"I'm not thinking anything. Geez. The world does not revolve around you, Maya."

Isabel had bigger things on her mind.

"Can we go to the clinic? I left my other notebook there," she lied.

"Fine," said Maya without looking at her.

When they arrived, Maya offered to let some of the animals into the yard for exercise. The veterinary assistant, Lisa, looked relieved to have some help. She was extremely busy today, just like Isabel had hoped. As Lisa turned away to help a customer, Isabel slipped the lab keys into her pocket.

Aunt Claire came into the office between patient visits to pick up a file.

"Hi, Izzie."

"Hi, Aunt Claire. We had to come by to get my folder, and Maya is helping with playtime."

"Great!" She picked up the file. "I have to go deal with a poor, sick kitty."

"I hope you can help."

She waited until Aunt Claire went into the exam room to sneak back into the lab. She slipped inside and kept the lights off. She went straight to Herbert and slipped him a treat, hoping he wouldn't give her away. She scratched Daisy behind the ear before walking over to the desk in the corner and powering on the computer.

OVER THE NEXT WEEK, attention shifted away from the research in their household because Maya's playoffs were about to start. Instead of practicing twice a week, she was with the team every day. Aunt Claire had been picking Isabel up from school and taking her to the clinic in the afternoons. Isabel didn't mind that one bit. In fact, she liked being able to spend more time helping there and less time arguing with Maya. She'd hoped Aunt Claire would tell her more about her research or let her hang out in the lab, but she hadn't.

Isabel took Nolan into the yard. He could fly but wouldn't go far. He was well trained and loyal. She sat in the grass and watched him fly in circles above the clinic.

The weather was beautiful, and the grass felt sticky on her palms as she leaned back. She remembered sitting in the grass like this one day, not that long ago. Their old house had a big backyard.

She sat in the grass, watching Dad and Maya play catch and enjoying the sunshine. Her mom had come to sit with her. They'd laughed as Dad struggled to even play catch at Maya's level.

"Do you think Maya will get a scholarship?"

"Maybe," Mom answered.

"She is really good. I wish I had that kind of talent."

Mom laughed loudly. "And your talents? What about those?"

Isabel shrugged.

"You know, Izzie, it takes all kinds of people and all kinds of abilities to do good in the world. I know being an athlete seems like the best possible thing when you're in middle school, but trust me, you are something very, very special."

Just then Nolan swooped down, breaking Isabel free from her memory. He dropped a dead rat at her feet.

"Err... thanks, Nolan, but you can have it."

Nolan used his beak to nudge the rat toward her.

She heard a laugh behind her.

"Part of being friends with predatory birds is accepting dead rats," Aunt Claire joked. "Don't be rude, you'll hurt Nolan's feelings. Grab it by the tail and let's go. I'm ready to close up for the day."

"Can we please visit with Daisy and Herbert?"

Aunt Claire sighed. "You know I don't want you too involved in this research, Izzie. It could get dangerous."

"Please, Aunt Claire? I'm never going to tell anyone about it. I just want to learn from you."

Aunt Claire thought it over, giving Isabel a concerned look.

"Okay fine. Take care of Nolan and meet me in there."

This time all the diagrams had been erased from the board. Everything looked neat and tidy. By the time Isabel walked in, both Herbert and Daisy were roaming around the lab. Aunt Claire was flipping through some notes on the table.

"I have a million questions about all this," Isabel said.

"So, do I. That's what research is, trying to answer questions, but just coming up with more and more along the way. That's the fun of it."

Isabel smiled. Aunt Claire was passionate about her work.

"Who is helping you with all of this? Lisa?"

"Actually no. I do all of this work on my own and report back data and findings to a team working on similar projects. We are spread out all over the world, but all part of the same team and we all get our funding from the same research grant."

"So, nobody else around here knows about Daisy or Herbert?"

"No, they don't. But don't worry, I take very good care of them myself."

"I know you do, but do you think they're lonely? Maybe we could take them home as pets. I can help take care of them."

"As nice as that would be, we can't. I need to keep them here so I can control what they are exposed to. It's important I know what and who they interact with, what they eat, and for Herbert, even what sounds he is exposed to."

"Well, Daisy is eating your printer paper."

Aunt Claire looked, then rushed over to Daisy to stop her.

"I've been thinking about this a lot." It was important Aunt Claire knew she was serious. "I want to help you."

"I know Izzie, but this is serious and important research."

"I know. I understand. But I think I can do it. I've been reading up a lot on genetic engineering. It doesn't make sense that Herbert can only say *no*. I think it's because it's the only word he's been trained to say. I could help train him. I can document everything I do and say. I can be useful."

Aunt Claire thought about that for a long time.

"You're right about the training. He does need exposure to additional vocabulary."

"Please, Aunt Claire. Let me help. I really want to be a part of this."

Aunt Claire nodded slowly.

"I will say *maybe*. Come up with a plan on exactly how you want to train him and how you plan to document it, and I will think about it. If it meets the parameters of my funding agreement, I will run it by the group, and if everyone—and I mean everyone—agrees it is a good idea, we will do it."

Isabel ran to Aunt Claire and squeezed her in a big hug.

"Thank you, Aunt Claire. I'm going to do a great job for you."

———

ISABEL HAD a hard time concentrating at school the next few days. She couldn't help but think her new research work was more important than learning about the history of Spain.

She was walking down the hallway toward programming class when she saw a group of girls standing close together. It sounded like one of them was crying. As she got closer, she realized it was Sara, and the other girls were picking on her.

"You're a loser, Sara. It's amazing you're even related to Andrew. I feel bad for him that he got someone so uncool as a sister."

The lead girl was Jessica Frane. She was a well-known bully, which must have come easy to her. Her family was rich, and she was beautiful. She always wore the coolest clothes and threw the most extravagant birthday parties. Everyone knew who she was. The other girls laughed. Sara kept her head down, weeping.

"I bet he's so embarrassed—"

"Hey!" Isabel surprised herself by jumping in. "Leave her alone."

"Oh look. Isabel Flores, another lame little sister. You two must stick together, huh? You can hang out in the shadows of your better siblings."

"What a stupid thing to make fun of us for. Having cool siblings. Isn't that a good thing?"

"It would be if either of you had anything worthwhile about yourselves, but you're both just dead weight. Your poor parents probably hate having to drag you along."

That was it. Isabel dove for Jessica, but someone grabbed her by the shoulders before she got close. She looked up to see Principal Reed.

"What's going on here?" she said.

"Nothing! We were just talking, and Isabel ran at me," said Jessica.

"It sounded like you were picking on her," the principal answered.

"No! Of course not! If anything, we were just giving each other a hard time."

The principal looked over at Sara, who was still teary-eyed.

"You'd all better come with me," she said and led them to her office.

Everyone clammed up in the principal's office. Isabel thought Principal Reed probably knew what was going on, but without anyone willing to complain, she couldn't punish anyone. Isabel was dismissed to programming class.

She stormed toward the classroom, furious over what Jessica had said. She walked in, sat at her table in the corner, and logged in. She didn't even bother trying to catch up on what Mr. Marcks was teaching.

Within minutes, she had hacked her way into Jessica's school file and was browsing for something she could use. It took some digging, but eventually she found the perfect thing. Jessica's picture from fourth grade, definitely an awkward phase for her. Her usual sleek, long blond hair was frizzy back then, and she had terrible bangs. She had braces and wore glasses, probably before she was able to put contacts in. Her skin was blotchy, too. She didn't wear make-up yet.

Isabel saved the photo to her desktop, then she found her way into the school directory and located the email distribution prompt. She added the photo to the email and typed "Jessica Frane should think twice before bullying other students. She's a fake." She hit send, sat back, and smiled.

IT ONLY TOOK ABOUT 15 minutes for Principal Reed to show up, out of breath and red in the face.

"Mr. Marcks, I need to see you outside immediately." She turned and stomped out the door.

She could hear them talking in tense voices.

"There's only one student capable of that kind of hacking," Isabel heard him say. Tavi turned around and gave Isabel a nervous look. This time Isabel did manage to smile at her.

Principal Reed stuck her head in the door and beckoned to Isabel. She knew it was coming. She'd already packed up.

She was asked to wait in a conference room in the administration office. It was terribly boring. After about half an hour, Principal Reed, Mr. Marcks, Aunt Claire and, to Isabel's surprise, a police officer walked in. A name plate pinned to his dark uniform said "Officer Williams." Isabel stared at it to avoid meeting his eyes.

Aunt Claire sat next to Isabel and gently rubbed her shoulder for a moment.

"Miss Flores, what you've done here is very serious," said Officer Williams. "Hacking is a crime, and hacking into the school's confidential records is a big deal."

Isabel hadn't really thought about it that way. Suddenly, she was terrified.

"I... I didn't... I..."

Aunt Claire squeezed her thigh and gently shook her head. Isabel stopped talking.

Principal Reed sighed. "Look Isabel, you should have told me about what happened with Jessica. I knew you had a problem, and I could have addressed it. This is completely out of hand."

"Perhaps you should have tried harder to address it," Aunt Claire said. "I understand this school has a zero-tolerance policy for bullying. If a student was bullying Isabel, and you knew about it, even saw it, shouldn't you have done something?"

Principal Reed pursed her lips together. "What Isabel did today is also bullying."

"Because she was being harassed in the hallways."

"Excuse me," interjected the officer. "Perhaps I can help here."

He turned to face Isabel.

"Isabel, what you did today was illegal, but we are going to let you off with a warning. It's very clear to us all, and frankly very impressive, that you have great skills here. I hope this experience encourages you to use those skills in positive ways. The police will be documenting this incident, and while it is a warning this time, cybercrimes are serious, and we will not be so lenient in the future."

Principal Reed sighed again. "The school is also going to give you a warning this time. You're a great student with no previous disciplinary problems, but please remember we consider both bullying and hacking to be extremely serious. I will not be lenient again."

They all stood up, and the adults shook hands as they walked out into the hallway. The officer was walking with Aunt Claire, chatting happily. *Is he flirting with her?* Isabel wondered.

"Isabel," Mr. Marcks leaned down and whispered. "Between you and me, that was some awesome programming work—it took me a long time to figure out how you got into the main email distribution system. It would be inappropriate for me to say I'm proud, but..." He squeezed her shoulders and walked away.

Isabel stood behind Aunt Claire and Officer Williams while they chatted and said goodbye. She followed Aunt Claire silently to the car.

"Thank you for standing up for me," Isabel whispered.

"Why didn't you tell Principal Reed that Jessica was picking on you, Izzie? Or why didn't you tell me? I could have helped you so you wouldn't get into this kind of trouble. You're very, very lucky the school isn't pressing charges against you."

She paused for a moment.

"It's probably because none of them are smart enough to really understand what you did." Aunt Claire tried to hide her smile by turning away.

"I know I shouldn't have done it, but Jessica was being so terrible. I thought she should have a taste of her own medicine."

"I can appreciate your sense of honor, Izzie, but this isn't the first time you've taken matters into you own hands. I mean, Maya's big game was only a few days ago."

Isabel looked down. She'd thought, foolishly, that Aunt Claire didn't know about that.

Aunt Claire's phone rang. She pushed the button to silence it.

"I don't want to discourage you from standing up for yourself, but I do need you to think about these things more carefully."

WHEN THEY ARRIVED at the clinic, Maya was nervously pacing outside. She rushed to Aunt Claire's window as they pulled into a parking space.

"Aunt Claire, Lisa told me to warn you."

Aunt Claire looked panicked. "What's wrong, Maya?"

"There's a man here, he won't leave. He said he wants to talk to you about your research. I think it is Dr. Rodriguez."

Aunt Claire's face tightened in anger.

"He came in asking to meet with you. We told him you weren't here, but he insisted on waiting. I tried to call you.

Lisa sneaked me out the back so I could tell you. What does he want, Aunt Claire?"

"I guess I'd better find out." She grabbed her purse and got out of the car. "Why don't you two head home? I'll bring home dinner in an hour or so."

She walked inside.

Isabel nodded her head to the left, toward the side of the building. Maya followed. She hunched down and crept under the windows, then sat down at the window to Aunt Claire's office, and a moment later, they heard voices approach.

FOUR

Nolan squawked, and Isabel worried he would give them away, but Aunt Claire was too distracted to notice.

"Claire, you and I both know how this is going to play out."

"Humor me, Steve. How is this going to play out?"

Steve chuckled. "We, at Gennovations, have funding far beyond yours. We have as many researchers as we could ever need. We have all the best equipment. We are going to solve this puzzle first, and we are going to solve it better."

"Humble as ever, aren't you?"

"Join us, Claire. Come on. Stop being so stubborn and come work with me."

Aunt Claire scoffed.

"I know how brilliant you are. Imagine if you had unlimited resources. What if you had 15 assistants tracking your results and data? What if you weren't bogged down with cleaning out kennels and helping sick kittens, Claire. This... all of this... is a waste of your talents."

"Steve, you have no idea what my talents are being used for. I happen to think my work here, even cleaning out kennels and helping sick kittens, is important and meaningful."

"I know, I get it. You love this work, too, but Claire, really, you are one of the foremost experts on genetics. You could be doing so much more at Gennovations. And I know this clinic pays the bills, but I could make your financial situation significantly better. You could send your nieces to the best schools on the planet, Claire. What about them?"

"I happen to think living in a loving household with some responsibilities is good for them, too. Do you have any idea how offensive you sound?"

"I am not trying to offend you. I'm trying to compliment you. You're the best. You know it. I know it. Come put that incredible brain to work."

"Thank you for your offer, Steve. Truly. I do appreciate it, but I am not interested."

Isabel and Maya looked at each other.

"Claire, when we publish our data first, which we will, all of your work will be moot. All of that research will be for nothing."

"Your confidence might just be your downfall, Steve."

Isabel heard her chair scrape backwards. She heard footsteps and then the door swung open.

"Thanks for stopping by, Steve. It's always a pleasure."

Isabel heard a second set of footsteps.

"You're making a huge mistake, Claire. I won't make this offer again."

"Goodbye, Steve."

"Suit yourself," he said.

Isabel and Maya scrambled back around to the front of the building just in time to see Dr. Rodriguez exit. He was a tall, handsome man with dark hair combed to one side. He wore a well-fitted suit and shiny shoes. He climbed into a Range Rover and sped out of the parking lot.

"Should we go back in?" Maya asked.

Isabel just glared at her.

"Okay, so no. I get it, Isabel."

ISABEL SAT in her room after dinner, going over what she'd heard again and again. She felt conflicted by it. She understood what Dr. Rodriguez was saying. Chances were, his big firm was more likely to make advances before Aunt Claire could. If she joined them, she would be able to work on research exclusively instead of working long days giving rabies shots to make sure the mortgage got paid. It made sense.

She thought of how Aunt Claire stood up for her at school today, though. How she understood Isabel and she did everything she could for her. She thought of how Aunt Claire had swooped in when Mom and Dad died and taken care of everything. She thought of the way people came into the clinic crying and Aunt Claire comforted them and helped. She wanted to help people, even if it cost her.

Isabel could hear Maya in the next room over, talking on the phone. The muffled sounds were occasionally broken up by giggles. She wondered who was on the other end of the phone. Maybe it was Andrew.

Isabel picked up her phone and got onto Instagram. She scrolled through posts from her friends back in Anaheim. She looked at their photos over the past few weeks, going about their lives without Isabel, as if she'd never been there.

She went to her own page and scrolled and scrolled. She had to go back a long way, but she made it. Photo after photo appeared of her happy life. She and Mom at the theater for a Christmas show. All four of them at one of Maya's softball games. Mom and Dad together at the beach. If she didn't think too hard, she could almost pretend this was still the way things were. She wondered, if Aunt Claire didn't have her and Maya to think about, would she have joined Gennovations? Would she have focused on her career instead of giving everything she had to creating a new "normal" for all three of them?

She scrolled back, remembering, until she fell asleep with the screen shining brightly on her face.

She'd wake up and reality would come back, but for tonight, she was back in time.

ISABEL AND AUNT Claire sat in the stands at the high school gym. Aunt Claire was wearing a Knights T-shirt and had a cheap purple pom-pom she kept pumping in the air. Isabel, on the other hand, couldn't muster that kind of enthusiasm. She was wearing jeans and a black hoodie, but at least this time she didn't have intentions of publicly embarrassing her sister.

Maya had been a nervous wreck all day. The school had never even been to the playoffs before, and now they were considered the favorite. Everyone knew it was mostly because of Maya. Isabel could not imagine that kind of pressure. She was grateful her hobby allowed her to sit behind a screen anonymously.

When the team took the court, the crowd cheered vigorously. Isabel decided that now was a good time to grab a snack.

"I'm going to the snack bar while the line is short," she announced.

"The game is starting. You don't want to miss it."

"I am sure I'll be able to see from there." She stood and began squeezing her way down the aisle.

As she turned her back on the game, she heard a huge cheer from the crowd. The Knights must have scored already. People were rushing to their seats as Isabel fought against the crowd, like a salmon swimming upstream.

She was right, no line at the snack bar. She walked up to see Sara behind the ordering window, playing on her phone. She almost turned away. They hadn't spoken since that day in the hallway.

"Hi Sara. Could I please have some chips and a Sprite?"

"Hey! Isabel!" Sara jumped up. "I've been looking for you." She looked around, checking that no one was paying any attention to them, then she locked eyes with Isabel.

"Thank you for standing up to Jessica for me at school."

"Oh yeah. Sure." Isabel brushed it off.

"No, really. Thank you for doing that. And I heard... well, I don't know if it's true... but I heard you sent that email..."

Isabel looked away.

"I won't ask. I don't want you to get in trouble. But if you did send it, you should know, the school has gone crazy about it. They brought in some consultant to fix their security problems I guess."

Isabel laughed. "How much are they paying this consultant? I would have done it for half."

"I knew it. How'd you learn to do all that anyway? It's $2.50." She handed Isabel her food.

Isabel smiled cleverly. "Thanks Sara. See you around."

Isabel had to admit, the game was exciting. It was close

until the very end, and once again, Maya had pulled off the win for her team. Aunt Claire had gone absolutely ballistic. Even Isabel caught herself cheering.

On the ride home, Aunt Claire dissected every play Maya made, going on and on about how amazing she was.

"Thank you, Aunt Claire. It was the whole team, though."

Aunt Claire's phone rang.

"Maya, can you get that?"

Maya answered the phone, and her face dropped. She looked at Aunt Claire with wide eyes.

"Hold on, please," she turned the phone away from her. "It's the police. Someone broke into the clinic."

THEY WERE all silent as Aunt Claire drove quickly to the clinic. It seemed to take hours to get there.

Two police cars with their lights flashing were parked outside. Aunt Claire and the girls rushed inside. The same officer from the school was waiting for them.

Nolan was squawking like crazy. Isabel rushed over and stroked his back feathers. Dogs barked from their kennels.

"Officer Williams," said Aunt Claire. "Thank you for being here. What happened?"

"We really aren't sure," he said. "Someone definitely broke in. The door has been forced open, but everything looks okay... to us, at least. We need you to take a look around."

Before he had finished his sentence, Aunt Claire was running to the lab. The girls followed, and the police were right behind them. Isabel could see why the police thought everything was fine—nothing appeared out of the place at all—but Aunt Claire's computer was gone. Someone had taken care to disconnect it from the network and stolen it.

Aunt Claire's face flushed, and her eyes were wide. She looked as if someone had smacked her.

Maya was on her hands and knees at the kennels. She was feeding treats to Herbert and Daisy, trying to keep Herbert from speaking. Isabel was relieved to see that the animals were there, unharmed.

"Claire," Officer Williams prompted.

"My... my computer is gone," she said. "It has a great deal of information saved on it."

"Okay, we will complete the report. Can we go into your office?"

"Izzie," Maya whispered. Isabel stepped closer. "Get the cops out of here before Herbert... you know."

Isabel walked up to the other officer, turning his attention away from the animals.

"Um, can we get you anything? Maybe, well, the break room has snacks."

"Thanks, dear, but I have to photograph the area where the theft occurred."

Maya looked at Isabel with wide eyes. She had to think quickly.

"Okay, then. My sister Maya and I are going to take these animals into the yard."

"Yes!" Maya said over-enthusiastically. "They need to go out!"

She opened the kennels and rushed Daisy and Herbert through the door.

"Good thinking," said Maya once they were outside. She looked at Isabel nervously. "Dr. Rodriguez?" she asked.

"Definitely," said Isabel.

AFTER THE POLICE had left and they locked the clinic back up as best they could, Aunt Claire, Maya, and Isabel drove silently home. Aunt Claire anxiously tapped on the steering wheel and looked around. Isabel felt nervous, too. She was watching behind them to make sure they weren't followed. When they got home, a police cruiser was waiting.

Aunt Claire rushed out. "What's wrong? Did they break into the house, too?"

Freddie was inside, barking like crazy.

"No, no, I'm sorry," said Officer Williams. "I was on my way back to the station when I realized it might be a good idea to make sure you got home okay."

Aunt Claire rubbed her forehead.

"I didn't mean to scare you. I apologize. I'll just have a quick look around. Considering how heated this dog is, I highly doubt anyone would have gotten in."

"Thank you," said Aunt Claire.

The doors were all locked, and the windows were closed tightly. Officer Williams looked all through the house and decided everything was fine. As he walked past the cockatoos, they fluffed up their crowns and puffed out their feathers.

"I really can't thank you enough for being so thorough," Aunt Claire said as she walked him out.

"No problem, Claire. Just give me a call if you need anything at all."

Officer Williams walked out, and Aunt Claire locked the door behind him.

She turned and leaned back against the door. Isabel and Maya were sitting on the couch. Aunt Claire walked over and sat between them.

"You girls did a really good job with Herbert and Daisy." Her voice cracked and her hands were shaking. "Thank you."

"I'm so sorry this happened, Aunt Claire," said Maya. "I can't believe it. It had to be Rodriguez, right? It was him."

"I'm sure it was," Aunt Claire sighed. "But I can't really tell the police that. If they started to dig in, everything could go public. It would become part of a public investigation. But I guess at this point, the data is out anyway, right? I mean all my research is gone. And it's in the hands of someone else."

"No," said Isabel. "It isn't."

FIVE

"What are you talking about Isabel? What do you mean?" Aunt Claire was speaking firmly. She was trying to hold back the excitement in her voice.

"I did something with the data," Isabel said. "I just had a bad feeling, so I wanted to keep it safe."

Aunt Claire and Maya stared at her silently, waiting for her to go on.

"A few days ago, while you were busy with patients, I sneaked into the lab. I backed up all the data onto my laptop. I brought it home."

"So, you have copies of everything? Is that what you're saying?"

"Yes. It's in my room."

Aunt Claire enveloped Isabel into a giant hug. Tears streamed down her face. "That was very wrong, but thank you so much, Izzie. Also, never do something like that again."

"Um, there's more actually."

Aunt Claire held her at arm's length.

"What? More what?"

"I encrypted the data on the hard drive of the computer they stole. I told you, I had a bad feeling."

"What does that mean, Izzie? Speak English!" said Maya.

"It means if someone turns on that computer and enters the wrong password, all of the notes, the records, everything, will turn into new characters."

"So, what, it becomes scrambled?" Aunt Claire prodded.

"No, actually." Isabel paused, wondering if she should go on. "I just changed every line of information to 'Do your own research, you money-hungry jerk.'"

Isabel smiled coyly.

After a moment of silence, Aunt Claire giggled. So did Maya. Soon the three of the were laughing hysterically on the couch.

"Wow, Izzie," said Maya. "Well done."

"WELL DONE!" yelled a cockatoo, and they both began to sing a terribly off-key song.

ISABEL RUSHED THROUGH HOMEWORK. She felt like she was close to a breakthrough with Herbert, and she was eager to get back to work.

She had a baggie of bacon in her backpack—real bacon she cooked herself, not just dog treats.

As soon as she finished her math assignment, she grabbed her laptop and her bacon and rushed into the lab. She gave Daisy a scratch behind the ear, then sat on the floor in front of Herbert.

She set up her computer to record their interaction so she could make notes about it later. She wanted to share the video and the information with Aunt Claire as soon as she had done something worthwhile.

With the computer set and bacon in her hand, she opened Herbert's kennel. He stepped out and she asked him to sit. She sat cross-legged, facing him. She looked him in the eye and said, "Stop." She paused. Herbert was silent.

"Stop," she said again.

Over and over again she tried, handing over a treat each time Herbert attempted to mimic her. It had been over an hour, and she was almost out of bacon when Herbert finally got it.

"Stop," said Isabel.

"Stop," said Herbert. Isabel cheered and threw her arms around Herbert. She gave him all the bacon she still had.

"Good boy, Herbert. Good boy. You did it!"

Isabel turned to the webcam on her computer.

"He did it," she told her future viewers, even though she knew that would only be her and Aunt Claire.

"Stop," said Herbert again, looking for more bacon.

"Oh sorry," said Isabel. She jumped up and ran for the treat jar on the counter. She fed him three treats.

"Stop," he said.

"Well, I guess I have to teach you what it means now, huh?"

Aunt Claire walked in.

"Aunt Claire! Perfect timing!"

Before Isabel could even prompt him, Herbert said, "Stop."

A huge smile grew across Aunt Claire's face.

"Wow. Great job, Herbert." She patted him on the head. "And great job, Izzie."

"I've recorded everything. I'm going to give you detailed notes, Aunt Claire."

"You made a lot of progress here."

She threw her arm around Isabel and gave her a squeeze.

Herbert nudged them both, looking for some affection, too.

AUNT CLAIRE PLANNED to pick Isabel up from school all week because Maya had extra volleyball practices. It was Friday, and Maya was going to be late tonight because her team had an away game. If they won this one, they would be playing for the district championship in a week. If they won that, they would play for the state title. Everyone was talking about it.

As Isabel walked out of programming class, she ran into Andrew. He usually waited in the parking lot for Sara. Isabel wondered if he'd started coming inside to protect Sara from bullies.

"Hey Isabel!"

Isabel nodded politely.

"Your sister was great in that game last week, huh?"

"Yeah, she's always great." Isabel stepped forward to walk past him.

"Hey, wait," he leaned down and whispered to her. "Thanks for helping Sara out. She really needs a friend like you."

Her phone buzzed in her hand. A text from Aunt Claire that she was running late. Isabel groaned.

"What's wrong?" Andrew asked.

"Nothing. My aunt is just running late."

"Well, I can give you a ride. I'm picking up Sara."

"You don't have to do that. I can wait here. It's no problem."

Sara came around the corner.

"We'd be happy to give you a lift. Really. Right, Sara?"

Sara's face brightened and she smiled at Isabel.

"Okay. Thanks."

Isabel pulled out her phone and texted Aunt Claire.

"Do you mind taking me to my aunt's vet clinic? That's where she is."

"Sure. That's on our way," Sara said.

The chill of fall was beginning to transition toward the cold of winter. All the orange leaves that previously decorated the parking lot were gone. Isabel pulled her collar tight around her neck.

As she was glancing around the trees, she noticed a gray van parked on the street, somewhat tucked behind the building. She thought she saw someone scramble out of the passenger seat.

Isabel pulled out her phone and took a picture. She zoomed in and took one of the license plate, too.

"What are you doing?" Sara asked.

"Have you ever seen that van before?" Isabel asked.

Andrew and Sara shook their heads.

"I'm sure it's nothing," Isabel said.

The ride to the clinic was surprisingly fun. The three of them talked and laughed all the way there. Isabel found herself thinking Sara had a great sense of humor.

When they pulled into the parking lot, Isabel grabbed her stuff and said goodbye.

"Wait a second," said Andrew, pointing to the front door. "Isabel, look at the door! The glass is broken!"

Isabel looked up, shocked.

There were no cars in the parking lot except Aunt

Claire's. Shattered glass littered the ground, and the door was ajar.

ISABEL FLEW from the car into the clinic. Andrew was behind her, yelling for her to wait. She swung open the door and gasped. Unlike the last break in, the place was destroyed. Chairs were knocked over, and papers were strewn everywhere. The glass on a picture in the lobby was shattered.

"Aunt Claire!" Isabel screamed, running toward the lab. "Aunt Claire, are you here?"

As Isabel ran through the clinic, she saw the back room and office were trashed. She burst into the lab. Aunt Claire was not there. Neither were Herbert or Daisy.

"Herbert! Claire! Daisy!" Isabel screamed their names over and over as she ran outside into the yard. It was empty.

She ran back into the lab. The computer was gone again, but this time so was everything else from the desk. The filing cabinet had been cleaned out, and every scrap of paper from the desk area had been removed.

Isabel felt the room spinning. It had to be Dr. Rodriguez again, but this time he went much further to get his hands on the data.

Andrew and Sara ran into the lab.

"You can't be in here," Isabel yelled. Then she looked around. *There's nothing to see anyway,* she thought.

"Isabel, are you okay? We've called the police. They're on their way."

Isabel felt dizzy. She needed to sit down.

"Maya," she said. "Call Maya."

THE POLICE ARRIVED MOMENTS LATER. They asked the three of them to wait outside while they looked around. Isabel insisted on taking Nolan out with her. He was squawking and trying to fly around, clearly distressed. Outside he swooped around in circles above the clinic.

Isabel let Andrew do the talking. The police listened carefully as he told them the circumstances of what they'd found.

Officer Williams was here again, talking to Andrew. He kept glancing at Isabel as they talked.

Finally, Maya arrived. She jumped from her car and ran to Isabel.

"Did you tell them anything?" she whispered.

"No, I know Aunt Claire wouldn't want me to, but what are we going to do? They kidnapped her, Maya."

Nolan flew by, swooping low. He perched on a nearby tree, watching them.

"We don't know that for sure yet. Maybe she's chasing them."

Isabel nodded. Isabel had tried calling Aunt Claire, but her phone went straight to voicemail, as she expected it would.

Maya walked over to Andrew and the police. Andrew gave her a warm hug.

Isabel realized Sara was close enough to have heard Maya, but Sara didn't ask any questions.

As Isabel stood there getting colder and looking at the beloved clinic, she started to panic. What if they did have Aunt Claire? What would they do with Herbert? What would happen to her and Maya if Aunt Claire was harmed?

Before she could lose herself completely, Officer

Williams beckoned her over. Sara held her by the arm and walked her to him.

"Okay girls, I sent Officer Gonzalez over to the house to check things out. If it is all clear, we will head back there. I need to take statements from both of you."

Officer Williams turned to Andrew.

"Thank you for your help. You and your sister can go now. Just give me your cell phone number in case we need anything."

Andrew did as he was told, then turned to Isabel.

"Do you want us to go to your house with you?"

"No, that's okay. You've already done so much. Maya and I will be fine."

Maya threw her arm around Isabel.

Andrew looked up at her.

"Call me if you need anything at all. And I'm sorry you had to miss the game."

Maya nodded politely. Suddenly Sara threw her arms around Isabel and gave her a tight hug. Then Andrew and Sara walked toward their car and were gone.

Isabel was desperate to talk to Maya alone. They needed to figure out what to do, but for now, that would have to wait.

Officer Williams got a call on the radio that the house was clear. He told the girls to get in his car.

"Actually, I can drive," said Maya. "We will just follow you there."

Officer Williams looked unsure.

"I know we are minors, and there is probably a rule, but it will be really hard for me to get my car back if we leave it here. Please, Officer, I promise to stay right behind you."

Officer Williams nodded, and the girls opened the car

doors. Just then, Nolan flew down and dropped a dead mouse on the police cruiser.

"That's his way of saying 'thank you,'" Isabel explained. She took Nolan back inside before they left.

———

"WHAT ARE we going to do, Maya?"

"I don't know. I'm trying to think."

"They kidnapped Aunt Claire. And they took Daisy and Herbert." Isabel felt tears welling in her eyes. "We have to help them."

"I know, Izzie. We will help them, but what's the best thing to do here? Should we tell the truth and try to get the police on our side, or would that make things worse? Aunt Claire is smart. She might have a plan. I don't know."

"I think we should tell them about Dr. Rodriguez. We don't have to say what the research is. We can just say he is a competitive researcher, and we know he is involved."

"Wait, Izzie. That's it. We can find him ourselves, can't we? We know who it is—we just have to figure out where he is."

Isabel started playing with the hem of her T-shirt. This could work if they could find him, but then what would they do?

"I bet Gennovations has a lot of security. I don't know if we'll be able to do anything."

Maya thought quietly for a few minutes. "Okay, how about this? Let's keep quiet for now, see what we can find. If we know where she is, we can always call the police at that time."

"We are going to have to shake Officer Williams. He's

not going to leave two minors alone with a possible kidnapper looking for them."

Maya nodded thoughtfully.

"That reminds me." Isabel pulled out her phone and displayed the picture of the van. "I saw this van at school today."

"Me, too. A van was parked outside the high school."

"Do you think they are watching us?"

"They must be."

A shiver went through Isabel. They were in danger, too.

"Do you really think Aunt Claire could be out chasing them?"

"No. Her car was still at the clinic," Maya sighed. Her forehead was wrinkled with worry. "I think they took her with them."

"Do you think this is my fault?"

"What? No. Of course not."

"Do you think I made them mad with my encryption and they came after her?"

"No, Izzie. I think they wanted her research, and when they couldn't get it—from her or by stealing it—they got desperate."

"Maya," Isabel said. "We are going to be okay, right?"

Tears welled in Maya's eyes. She turned to look at Isabel.

"I don't know."

SIX

Officer Williams parked on the street in front of the house. Maya pulled into the driveway. Everything looked perfectly normal to Isabel, but even knowing that Officer Gonzalez had checked it out, she was nervous to go inside.

Maya unlocked the door, and they went in.

"Make yourselves comfortable," said Officer Williams. "If you want to change your clothes or grab a snack or anything, I can wait."

"No, that's okay," said Maya. She gestured for him to sit on the couch. "You can take our statements now."

Isabel was nervous. She did not want to mess this up. She felt like Aunt Claire was counting on her.

"Maya, let's start with you. You were not present when the break-in was discovered. Can you tell me about the last time you were at the clinic? Did you see anything unusual?"

Maya talked in normal even tones. She told Officer Williams all about her normal day, her normal routine. She told him how she had been there less frequently because of the volleyball playoffs. Maya didn't have to lie much.

Officer Williams turned to Isabel. The last time Isabel

was at the clinic, she'd taught a dog to say a new word. She had no choice but to lie.

"Nothing unusual," she said.

She wasn't sure if Officer Williams was buying it. He asked about today, and she remembered the text from Aunt Claire. The one about running late.

Officer Williams looked at her phone.

"Hmm. That text seems pretty normal. I think it's safe to assume she wasn't in any trouble at that point."

Officer Williams noted the time of the text in his notebook.

"We have tried searching for her cell phone, but it's turned off so we can't track it," he added.

"There's something else. Something I noticed that was unusual."

She told him about the van she saw at school. Isabel showed him the pictures.

"This could be a coincidence, but we will check it out. Excuse me a moment." He stood up and began talking into his radio, asking them to run the license plate.

"What are you doing? Why did you tell him that?" whispered Maya.

"First of all, to throw them off and give them something to look for. A van creeping around sounds like a petty criminal, not a multimillion-dollar research corporation. But also, maybe they can lead us to the van."

Officer Williams returned and told them they were searching for the van.

"I can't leave you two unaccompanied, and Child Services can't get anyone here until the morning at best."

"So, you're staying here?" Isabel asked.

"I'm afraid not. It's a violation of policy to stay here overnight with you. I can bring you back here tomorrow, but

I'm going to have to take you two down to the station for the night."

Maya looked horrified. "The jail?"

"No, you don't have to stay in the jail. We have a little room set up with cots for when officers have to stay on long shifts. You can stay in there."

Isabel was furious. She just wanted to get to her room, to her computer. She needed to know if she could find anything on Gennovations. She needed to help Aunt Claire. Then she had an idea.

"Can we bring a few things?"

"Sure, pack whatever you'd like. We aren't in a hurry."

Isabel dashed up to her room and grabbed her laptop, a collection of various cables, and a book with a blacked-out cover.

When she came out, Maya and Officer Williams were waiting for her.

———

"YOU CANNOT BE SERIOUS, ISABEL." Maya whispered harshly. "This is not a good idea."

Isabel ignored her and kept at her work. They were in a small room with two cots and nothing else. An overhead florescent light shined harshly from above. Isabel was sitting on the floor. She had the laptop propped up on the cot and the open book in her lap. Maya was pacing the few steps she could in the tiny room.

"Isabel. Listen to me. You cannot hack into the police department's network."

Isabel smiled slyly and slowly turned her head toward her sister. "I just did."

Maya's eyes went wide. She looked at the screen and

saw that Isabel's laptop mirrored the desktop image of all the computers they had walked by on the way in.

"You are scary good at this," Maya added. "I didn't mean you *couldn't* do it. I meant you *shouldn't* do it. Can you imagine what kind of trouble you could get in for this?"

"Probably less trouble than Aunt Claire is currently in."

Maya inhaled sharply, and tears welled in her eyes. She sat quietly while Isabel began to look through files. Nothing caught her eye, so she loaded one of the department's search tools and began to search for things like *Gennovations* and *Dr. Rodriguez.*

"I found something," she said. "There are some county records showing a building owned by Gennovations Incorporated just outside of town. It's in the foothills. I think it's county land."

"Do you think that's where Aunt Claire is?"

"It's possible." Isabel pulled up the location on Google Earth. It was not just a building, but a massive complex with lots of buildings, a huge wall, and a guarded gate at the entrance. "It would be pretty easy to keep someone in there."

"And hard to get in," Maya answered.

Isabel tried to do a street view of the building, but Google did not have the imagery. Clearly, they weren't allowed on the property.

"Oh, I know," she said. She closed a window and pulled up a database from the county. "I bet I can find their building plans."

Sure enough, a few minutes later, the girls were looking over the blueprints of the buildings that Gennovations owned.

"I just wish we knew for sure that Aunt Claire was in there," said Maya.

"I would guess she is. Unless she's doing what we are doing right now and trying to get in herself."

"But she wouldn't turn her phone off, would she?"

That gave Isabel another idea. "I can't track the phone if it's off, but I could probably see where it was used last."

It took a while but eventually Isabel was able to look at what towers Aunt Claire's phone had pinged that day. The very last call was north of them, toward the Gennovations facility.

"So, they either kidnapped her and she tried to call for help, or she went willing and... I don't know... her phone died," Maya said.

Isabel was silent for a moment. Tears welled in her eyes.

"What's wrong, Isabel?"

"This is my fault. If she got kidnapped and if anything bad happens to Daisy and Herbert, it's because of me."

"What? Why would you say that? It's because of the research."

"No. The first time they came in gently and took the computer. They didn't hurt anyone or break anything. But I made them mad by encrypting the data. That's why they broke everything and left a huge mess. It's my fault."

Maya stared at her helplessly.

"We've got to do something." Isabel fumed.

"Maybe we need to tell the police what we know," said Maya softly.

"We can't. We can't let them in on Aunt Claire's research. It will ruin her life's work."

"What if her life is in danger, Isabel? Isn't that more important here?"

Isabel sat down on the cot. Maya was right, but Isabel was not ready to give up yet. "We have to at least try on our own, Maya. We have to give it a shot. If we can't help, if we can't do this, then we will tell the police everything."

Maya nodded slowly. "Okay. That's fair. But how exactly do we try to help her when we are stuck in here?"

Isabel smiled. "Andrew."

"What?" Maya's eyes were wide.

"Text Andrew. Ask him if he will pick us up here and take us to Aunt Claire's clinic. He will."

Maya stared back at her sister. "I'm not sure—"

"Make sure you tell him we will meet him outside. We don't want him to come in."

ISABEL HAD PACKED up her stuff and turned out the lights. She wanted everyone to think they'd gone to sleep for the night. A few minutes before they expected Andrew (*and hopefully Sara*, thought Isabel) they slowly and silently opened the door to the hallway. The officer who was supposed to be watching them was hunched over the computer at his cubicle, hard at work. They tiptoed past. They had to walk across the dispatch office into another hallway with a door that opened off the side of the building. They waited until the phone rang and the dispatcher was busy with a 911 call to creep past her. Isabel went first and made it to the dark hallway.

As Maya crossed, the dispatcher turned and saw her.

"Are you lost, sweetie?"

"Oh... um... no... I..." Isabel stared at Maya wide-eyed. "I'm just stretching my legs. Big practice tonight, you know, for the volleyball team. My quads are just really tight."

"Oh okay, sweetie. Well, you girls just let me know if you need anything."

"Thank you, ma'am." She continued down the hall.

Isabel heard the woman whisper "sweet girl" as they walked away.

They opened the door very quietly and slipped out.

"I can't believe we just sneaked out of a police station," said Maya.

"Good thing this is a little, crime-free town," said Isabel. "We never could have done that in Anaheim."

Andrew was waiting for them in the parking lot. He smiled widely when he spotted them. Sara popped out from the passenger seat and waved.

"Thanks for the ride," said Maya.

"No problem. I'm happy to help. Although I will say I was surprised the police wouldn't take you back to the clinic themselves."

Maya looked at Isabel.

"They're just so busy, you know, working the case. We told them we could call some friends so they could keep at it."

Maya and Andrew climbed into the front seats. Isabel and Sara climbed into the back.

"I'm sorry about all this," Sara said. She reached out and touched Isabel's knee, comforting her. Isabel smiled back.

As he drove, Andrew asked a lot of questions. Maya answered as best as she could without telling him about the research. When they were about to turn into the parking lot, Isabel noticed something move on the side of the building.

"Don't turn!" she shouted. "Keep driving!"

Andrew immediately complied.

"What is it?" Maya asked.

"The van. It's parked at the clinic."

SEVEN

They drove slowly around the corner to get a better look. The van was parked in the shadows, and no one was around it. Isabel pulled out her phone and took a few photos.

"I guess we should call the police again," asked Andrew.

"No!" shrieked Maya. "Um, I mean, no thank you. They already know about the van."

Isabel remembered the police were supposed to be looking for it.

"Actually, yes," she said. Maya glared at her. "Just, um, maybe don't mention that we are with you." She smiled nervously.

"What do you mean?" Sara asked.

"Just, you know, say you were driving by and saw a suspicious van outside the clinic. They'll check it out."

"Do the police think you're still at the station?" Sara asked.

"Um. It's kind of a long story," said Isabel. She smiled mischievously, and Sara stared at her with her mouth open.

Andrew shook his head and pulled out his phone. Exactly as Isabel had asked, he told the dispatcher he was driving by when he saw the van parked outside the clinic. They said they'd send someone over right away.

"So, um, maybe we could go somewhere else," Maya said.

"Like that diner." Isabel pointed to a diner across the street from the clinic. It had an open booth against the window with a perfect view.

MAYA AND ISABEL could not peel their eyes from the windows. They'd ordered shakes, then burgers, then pie. They were taking as long as possible to eat it. Andrew and Sara had long since finished.

This plan had definitely backfired. The police had been in the clinic parking lot for over an hour. It didn't seem like they had learned much from the van driver. They'd taped off the parking lot, too. It sure didn't look like they could get inside anytime soon.

The waitress, who had set the bill on the table 20 minutes ago, kept giving them dirty looks.

"So... do you guys want to go over there or what?" Andrew asked.

Isabel pursed her lips and looked at Maya.

"We just really want to stay out of their way," said Maya. "You guys can go if you want. We'll just wait here. Thanks for the ride."

Andrew eyed her suspiciously. Sara stared at Isabel.

"You can't go to the clinic because the police think you're at the station, and you sneaked out," Sara said.

Isabel slouched down in her seat. Maya took a deep breath.

"We just really need to look around," she finally said.

"Why? What's going on here? Did you guys have something to do with the break-in?" Andrew asked sternly.

"No. It's not that. It's just that we... well... we might know more about it than we told the cops, and we really need to check something out."

"Check what out?"

"We can't really say," Isabel jumped in. "It's, unfortunately, really important that we keep it a secret. That's why we haven't told Officer Williams. It's not that we are trying to be deceitful. We are trying to do the right thing. Whatever that is."

"Then we'll help you," Andrew stated. "What do you need?"

"Really," Isabel asked. "Just like that?"

"Just like that," he smiled widely.

"Okay. New plan." Isabel leaned in and whispered to the others.

THE RIDE OUT to Gennovations was long, and no one had much to say. As they approached the location, Isabel could see lights out in the distance. She could tell this facility would be huge.

As they approached, it became obvious they would be seen if they drove much closer.

"Andrew, can you please pull over. I don't think we can get much closer without them noticing us," said Isabel.

Andrew pulled over. "You're right. We can't see much from here."

"We can go on foot," said Maya.

"Why don't we just drive up to The Point?" Sara asked.

"The Point? What's that?" Isabel asked.

"You know, The Point. The place up the hill where everyone goes to make out in their cars."

Andrew looked dumbfounded. "Why do you know about that?"

"Why don't *you* know about it?" she mocked.

Maya laughed, then caught herself when Andrew gave her a dirty look. "Sorry," she mumbled.

"Relax, Andrew, I've never actually been there."

"Do you know how to get there?" asked Isabel.

"There is a turnout off Depot Road," Andrew said. "I'm not actually sure if it faces that direction, but it's worth a shot, I think."

"So, you *have* been there," Sara said with a giggle.

Andrew blushed and stared straight out the windshield. He turned the car around and headed for the Depot Road turn. He drove slowly up the winding road, being careful not to miss a lookout point. As they came around a corner, a clearing opened up along the left side of the road. The area had lots of tall trees on either side of it. It was a dirt patch big enough for two or three cars, but it was empty now. It faced right toward the Gennovations building. Andrew turned off his headlights and stopped the car. Isabel and Sara climbed out of the car for a better look since they were in the back seat.

It was cold and dark. Isabel wrapped her arms around herself. She had a perfect view of the Gennovations facility, and it was intimidating.

The entire place, inside the high block wall, was lit up brightly. A small guard shack sat in front of a big gate off the main road.

Four buildings made up the complex, one much larger than the others, plus a lot of natural forest within the walls. Isabel remembered this from the blueprints she'd found, but she hadn't studied them closely enough to know what each building was for.

"Do you think your aunt is in there?" Sara asked.

"Yes. I just hope she's in there because she went with them, not because they took her."

"Do you think she may have wanted to go?"

"I think, if it came down to protecting her animals and her research, she would go, but I can't believe she wouldn't have contacted us."

Sara nodded and stared down at the huge Gennovations complex. "Do you know what that place is? People always talk about it being some kind of factory or something."

"It's not a factory. It's a research facility."

"What kind of research do they do there?"

Isabel paused.

"We'd better go. I don't think we are going to be able to get in there," Isabel said instead of answering Sara's question. "Maya and I need a new plan."

They turned around to walk back to the car. Maya was crying in the passenger seat, and Andrew had his arm around her.

Sara and Isabel looked at each other.

"It's been a hard day," said Isabel.

Sara nodded, and they got back in the car.

"NOW WHAT?" said Maya. "We can't really sneak back into the police station."

Isabel found it hard to believe the police weren't calling them by now. They must really believe they were sleeping in that room.

"I don't know, but we need a plan. A lot of plans, actually. I have no idea how to get inside that facility," Isabel said as they drove back down the dark road toward town. Isabel was worried now. Dr. Rodriguez hadn't scared her, but seeing Gennovations' sprawling facility with walls and guards changed that. She wondered what animals might be kept in there and what Gennovations might be doing to them. She thought of Herbert and Daisy.

"Is that place, like, a vet, too?" asked Andrew.

"Not exactly." Maya said.

"But are there animals there?"

"More than likely."

"I might know how to get us in, then," said Andrew. "It's going to sound crazy, though."

"We're listening," said Isabel.

"Our parents own the feed store, you know," Andrew started.

"Yes!" shouted Sara. "Andrew, you're a genius."

Andrew smiled widely. "We will just have to make a delivery."

As they pulled back into town, Maya suggested they drive by the clinic first to see if the police and van were still there. They were gone.

"We can't sneak in with a delivery in the middle of the night," said Maya. "Let's go home, and we'll figure out how to explain what we did later."

"Call us in the morning. We'll come over and make a plan."

Sara reached out and squeezed Isabel's hand. Isabel smiled back at her.

WEARY AND SLOW, Maya and Isabel walked into the house. The cockatoos greeted them, "HELLO! HELLO!"

Isabel stopped to pet them as she walked by.

Freddie bounded up to them, then immediately ran to his food dish and started to whine. Maya said she'd take care of it. Isabel headed for her room. Her legs were heavy, and she could feel sleep nagging at her. She was worried for the animals and for Aunt Claire, but right now, she was too tired to even think straight. She turned on the light in her room and screamed. Maya came running in.

Daisy was standing in the room, chewing on the Isabel's comforter.

"How on Earth did you get here?" Isabel sat on the floor next to Daisy and began scratching her behind the ear. Something was stuck under her collar. Isabel pulled out a note and her mouth dropped open. She looked up at her sister.

"Well?" said Maya.

Isabel turned the note around so Maya could read it. "Get help! Go to the police and tell them everything!"

They were both silent for a moment. Tears ran down Isabel's cheeks.

"She must really be in trouble," said Isabel.

Maya pulled her phone from her pocket and dialed Officer Williams.

EIGHT

Officer Williams was not pleased when he learned the girls had sneaked out of the station.

"We were just so tired," Maya lied. "We wanted to sleep in our own beds."

"We are trying to protect you. This is for your own safety."

Another officer who had responded with Officer Williams stood, hanging his head. Obviously, he was taking the fall for the girls sneaking out.

"Never mind that!" shouted Isabel. "What about this?!"

She held the note out to Officer Williams. He took the note from her and sat on the couch.

"So, you got this from your pet goat?"

"Yes. But Daisy isn't a regular goat. She's able to produce milk that has medicinal purposes."

"Her milk has medicine in it?" Officer Williams looked skeptical.

"Yes. And Herbert, the dog who is missing, he can talk."

Officer Williams pursed his lips together. His eyebrows came together and down.

"It's all part of Aunt Claire's research. She is working on a research grant, and Dr. Rodriguez stole her data and kidnapped her."

"Isabel, slow down," Maya tried to cut in. She could see that Officer Williams was growing frustrated.

"This is not a joke, young lady," said Officer Williams.

"I know it's not a joke. Of course, it's not a joke. Our aunt is missing, and I'm trying to tell you where she is. You are the one who needs to take this seriously."

Isabel was standing over Officer Williams now. She clenched her hands into fists and ground her teeth together.

"You want me to believe your aunt and her talking dog were kidnapped by a doctor?"

"Yes. Because that's what happened."

"That is science fiction."

"SCIENCE FICTION! SCIENCE FICTION! SCIENCE FICTION!" the cockatoos squawked suddenly, startling everyone.

That was all Isabel could take. She stormed from the living room into her bedroom with Daisy, slamming the door behind her. She stomped all over the room, unable to sit down. Her hands shook as she grabbed a book from her desk and threw it across the room as hard as she could, putting an unsightly dent in the wall.

———

ISABEL COULD HEAR the frustration rising in Maya's voice as she tried, much more calmly, to explain the situation to Officer Williams in the living room. Isabel sat on the floor of her bedroom with her back against the door. Daisy was laying down next to her, letting Isabel scratch behind her ears.

"I wish you could talk, too, Daisy. I need to know where you've been and how you got here."

A gentle knock sounded at the door.

"Isabel," said Maya. "Can you come out here?"

Reluctantly, Isabel stood up. She walked silently into the living room and stood with her arms across her chest.

Officer Williams explained that Child Protective Services was unable to get there, so they had made an exception to their policy and would allow the girls to stay in the house tonight, as long as an officer was with them. They would be taking shifts and checking in frequently.

"Are you going to look for Aunt Claire?" Isabel snapped.

Officer Williams rubbed his forehead. "That's the only thing I've done since you called me this afternoon."

He looked from Maya to Isabel, and his posture softened.

"Look girls, I know you are scared and frustrated, but we are doing the best we can. I will follow up on what you told me."

Isabel scoffed.

"I will. You have my word."

"Thank you, Officer," said Maya.

He nodded at them and turned to leave.

"Please. Puh-*leeze* do not leave the house tonight. I have a limited number of officers. I simply don't have the manpower to look for your aunt *and* chase you two around."

"We won't," said Maya.

"Should I order you a pizza or something?"

"We can take care of it," Maya answered.

Officer Williams nodded to them once more and walked out. The officer assigned to babysit them stood at attention near the door, overcompensating for his slip-up earlier. He locked the door behind Officer Williams.

Isabel turned on her heel and headed for her room. Maya followed.

"What?" Isabel snapped.

"Geez! I just wanted to tell you what I told him."

"Does it matter? He doesn't believe us, anyway. I don't know why you wasted your breath."

"Because I am trying to help. Maybe if you could have talked to him without throwing a temper tantrum, he would have believed you."

"You think he believes you? Come on Maya, you're smarter than that."

"Well at least I tried, Isabel. At least I did something."

Maya stormed down the hall to her room and slammed the door. Isabel could hear her crying in her room.

THE SUN WAS ABOUT to come up, and Isabel had hardly slept at all. Maybe Maya was right, she should have been calmer when she talked to Officer Williams. Maybe he would have believed her if she would have started slower.

"I really prefer animals and computers to people," she told Daisy.

Isabel picked up the note from her nightstand and studied it. Something about it really bothered her. She stood up and peeked out her bedroom door. The officer was sitting on the couch, playing a game on his phone. Isabel slipped quietly out her door and down the hall to Maya's room. She opened the door a crack. It was still dark inside.

"Maya," she whispered. "Are you awake?"

"Yeah. Come in."

Isabel stepped into the room and walked over to the bed. Maya was tucked in under the covers but wide awake. She leaned over and turned on the lamp on her nightstand.

"Look at this again." She handed Maya the note, and Maya stared at it.

"What?"

"It's not Aunt Claire's handwriting."

Maya looked at it for another moment.

"You're right."

"It's funny. I keep thinking that if Aunt Claire wasn't kidnapped, if she were running around trying to stop Dr. Rodriguez, she would never leave us hanging. She would have contacted us or something."

Maya nodded. Her eyes were wide.

"She would have known they couldn't leave us alone. We're minors. She is smart enough to know we'd be stuck."

"And she would want our help."

"Well, maybe."

"And she could have just gone to the police herself, right? I mean, they'd have believed her. So, *she* didn't bring Daisy here. She didn't leave this note. She couldn't have."

"So, who did?"

NINE

The next morning, Officer Williams came by again. He relieved the officer who had been there overnight and brought someone new. Maya explained the note to him.

"So, who do you think brought the goat here?"

Daisy had wandered in, chewing a washcloth. Isabel shook her head.

"We don't know," said Maya. "We were hoping it might help your investigation though."

He pulled a plastic baggie out of his pocket and put the note inside.

"We probably won't be able to get any prints off of it, but we will see."

Isabel couldn't decide if he was really going to test it or if he was just placating them. Maya seemed very confident Officer Williams would take care of everything.

"Look, girls," he said. "I'm sorry about last night. I was very upset you had left the station. You could be in danger, and I need to keep you safe. I promise I am doing everything I can to get to the bottom of this."

Isabel sat down and rested her hands in her lap. "So, you believe us?"

"I believe something pretty strange is going on." He looked over at Daisy. "When I leave here, I'll drive out to the Gennovations facility and see what I can find out."

Isabel stood back up.

"We can go with you. We can help. We know what Dr. Rodriguez looks like. And Herbert knows me, of course."

Officer Williams shook his head.

"No, Isabel. You cannot come with me. This is a police investigation. You and your sister may be at risk. We have no idea what is in that facility."

Isabel began to protest. Maya put her hand firmly on her sister's shoulder.

"We understand," said Maya.

"I will keep you updated. If I find out anything new, you will be the first to know. Meanwhile, stay home. Officer Darnel will stay with you."

"I feel good about this," Maya said after Officer Williams walked out. "He will find her."

Isabel nodded, debating how she would spend the next few hours without going stir crazy.

"HI ANDREW," Maya spoke into her phone a few hours later. "We are doing okay, thanks... yeah, things have changed a bit... can you hold on?"

Maya stood up from the couch and walked into her room; she cocked her head to the inside indicating to Isabel she should follow. Isabel closed the door behind her, and Maya put Andrew on speaker. She sat down on the floor next to Maya's bed. She plucked a picture off Maya's nightstand of them with Mom and Dad. Isabel looked up at herself. She was smiling widely in the picture. She wished Dad were here now to throw his arm around her like that.

"Okay, I'm in my room with Isabel. You're on speaker."

"Hi Isabel," Sara piped up in the background. Andrew laughed.

"Obviously, Sara is here, too."

"We are at the house with a police guard," Maya explained. "We have a babysitter after breaking out of the station. We told the police everything we know, and they are investigating."

"Oh, that's good. So... will you tell us what you know?"

Maya looked at Isabel and shrugged her shoulders.

"It's really a pretty complicated story," said Isabel. "Maybe it would be easier to explain in person."

"We'll come over." Sara chirped in.

Isabel was surprised again at their willingness to be involved. She wondered what Officer Darnel would think of having houseguests.

"See you in ten," Andrew said.

Maya and Isabel walked back into the living room.

"Excuse me, Officer Darnel. We have some friends coming by. Is that okay?"

"What kind of friends?"

"Friends from school. Andrew and Sara Banks."

"Oh. I know the Banks kids," he smiled. "I'll call it in so, if someone sees their car outside, they won't worry. Is Andrew driving?"

He spoke into his radio. When Andrew and Sara arrived, they greeted the officer. He asked about their parents. Andrew told him they were out of town, and he said he remembered them saying they'd be traveling this week. Sometimes, Isabel was amazed by what a small town this really was. The cockatoos shouted until Andrew and Sara walked over and petted their crowned heads.

"It's good to see all of you kids, but it's time for shift change. I'm going to brief the new officer."

"We'll be in my room," said Maya.

SARA AND ANDREW stared at Isabel and Maya with their mouths hanging open.

"So anyway, Officer Williams is at Gennovations now," Maya finished. "He will find something for sure."

Andrew nodded slowly. Sara opened her mouth to say something, then closed it again.

"Sorry we didn't tell you everything last night," said Maya. "We just didn't know if we should, but now that we've told the police, I'm sure it won't stay a secret much longer. I just hope Aunt Claire doesn't lose her funding or anything."

"So... the dog... he really talks?" Andrew asked.

"He can only say two words. It's not like he has a whole conversation. I mean, these cockatoos say a lot more than Herbert ever will."

"And the goat really has medicine in her milk. I mean, that's weird."

Daisy nosed around the kitchen looking for something to eat, unfazed that she was being discussed.

"Aunt Claire is truly brilliant," said Isabel. "She really sees this as a way to help people. I think she is probably further ahead on this than any other researcher. That's why Dr. Rodriguez is after her."

Andrew and Sara were silent for a while, processing this

information. It occurred to Isabel how willing they had been to help them, even before they knew why.

"I just wish Officer Williams would hurry up and get back here," said Maya. "I'm ready for this whole thing to be over. At least it's the weekend, and I don't have a game until Monday."

Isabel rolled her eyes. How could Maya care at all about a stupid game at a time like this?

Having Andrew and Sara over made the waiting a lot more bearable for Isabel, though she still felt anxious. Maya, on the other hand, seemed completely carefree. *She really thinks Officer Williams is going to solve this mystery today,* thought Isabel.

Unfortunately, Maya was wrong.

Officer Williams walked in a few hours later. His face had creases Isabel hadn't seen before. He sighed heavily and sat down on the couch. All of them waited, staring at him intently.

"Well," Maya finally said. "Did you find her?"

"Gennovations was ready for me," he started. He explained that when he arrived at the facility he was greeted by their head of security and a lawyer. They took him inside and carefully monitored his every move, so he was not able to look around. They also stopped him from talking to Dr. Rodriguez. They told him the work being done at the facility was extremely confidential, and without a warrant, he would not be allowed to investigate. It had basically been a colossal waste of time.

"So, get a warrant," Isabel said.

"It's not that easy. I don't have any real evidence that Dr. Rodriguez is involved, and I certainly don't have anything on Gennovations. I'm sorry, but no judge is going to grant me a warrant based on a conversation where two teenage girls overheard a man offer their aunt a job."

Isabel wasn't surprised that the police were no help, but Maya looked devastated.

"But she's in there," Maya said. "We know she is. And she is in danger. And YOU are the police."

Officer Williams nodded sadly.

"What now?" Andrew asked firmly.

"We continue to investigate the case based on the clues we found at the crime scene."

"And what clues did you find at the crime scene?" Isabel asked.

"There were fingerprints and shoeprints we can look into."

"Hundreds of people have walked all around the clinic and touched things. What good is that going to do? I mean, Lisa's fingerprints are probably on every surface in that building."

Then it hit her... Lisa. Where was Lisa? She would have been at the clinic that afternoon, and, as far as Isabel knew, no one had heard from her at all.

TEN

"Let's play a computer game." Isabel shouted as soon as Officer Williams left. "Come on guys." She smiled sweetly. Maya looked confused.

The other three dashed into Isabel's room after her. She didn't acknowledge them, except to tell Sara to close the door. Isabel sat down in front of her laptop; her eyebrows were drawn together in concentration. She began typing furiously. She paused, bit her lip, and started again. Andrew and Sara looked at each other and then at Maya, who just shrugged.

Finally, Isabel sat back in her chair and took a deep breath. A small smile spread across her face.

"What are you up—" Maya started to ask. She was interrupted by a gentle knock on the door.

The officer opened the door slowly and stuck his head in the room.

"Hey kids," he said. "There's been an emergency, and I've been called away, but another officer is on his way and will be here in two minutes. You'll be alone for just a minute. Will you be okay?"

"Yes," said Isabel. "We will be fine. I'll follow you and lock the door."

Isabel stood and walked through the room. The others looked at her with confused expressions.

Seconds later, she returned.

"Okay, let's go," she said.

"What just happened?" said Maya.

"You heard him. He got an important message and was called away," Isabel said.

Realization crossed Maya's face, and her eyes went wide.

"Did you send that message?" she shrieked.

Isabel just shrugged and began packing a backpack with tech gear.

"Isabel, seriously, this is a really bad idea," Maya said.

"We have to get out of here," Isabel said matter-of-factly. She slung the backpack over her shoulder. "Andrew, Sara, you don't have to do this. You guys can go home. I don't want to get you in trouble or put you in any kind of danger."

Andrew and Sara looked at each other.

"We're with you," said Sara.

"Honestly, this is the most exciting thing that's ever happened in this town," Andrew added. "We wouldn't want to miss it."

"And you?" Isabel looked at Maya. She crossed her arms in front of her and looked around, avoiding eye contact with Isabel.

"YOU! YOU!" squawked one of the cockatoos. "AND YOU!"

"Let's go," she said.

"We'd better take my car," said Andrew. "Less obvious."

"Where are we going anyway?" asked Sara.

"Lisa Harris's house."

WHEN THEY KNOCKED on Lisa's door, no one answered. The TV was on inside, and there were two cars in the driveway.

Maya peeked in the window but did not see anyone.

"Knock again. They're home."

After several more minutes of knocking, the door creaked open a bit.

"You have to go," Lisa whispered through the crack. "Get out of here. Now. Go away."

"Why, Lisa? What's going on? Are you okay?"

Lisa blew air out of her cheeks. She opened the door more and peered around outside.

"Do you think you were followed?"

"Followed? What on earth are you talking about, Lisa? No, we weren't followed."

"Get inside. Hurry!"

She took one more quick look up and down the street before closing and locking the door. Inside, the house was perfectly normal and suburban. Baby toys were strewn around the living room floor. Lisa's new baby was sleeping in his swing. A laundry basket full of clothes occupied the loveseat. Lisa's husband was standing at the end of the room, looking very unfriendly.

"This is not a good idea, Lisa," he said sternly.

"What is going on?" Maya asked.

"You shouldn't be here. They told me they would hurt my family." Lisa's eyes darted around the room, and she started to sweat. "Girls, you are in danger. You must go to the police. They have Claire, and you need help. But you cannot tell them I know."

"Why? What happened?"

Lisa took a deep breath. Her husband shook his head.

"Okay, listen, you can't ever tell the police or anyone else I told you this. If you do, my whole family is in a lot of danger. A bunch of men came into the clinic. They tied us up and went into the lab. They took everything they could find. They took Daisy and Herbert. They threw us in a van and drove for a while. As soon as we got there, they separated us."

Lisa's husband stormed out of the room.

"It only took a few minutes for them to realize I didn't know anything. I truly didn't. I think Claire told them that, too. They didn't see anything special with Daisy, either. They blindfolded me, brought us home, and told me if I ever, ever told anyone about this, they would hurt my family." She started to cry. "They said they'd be watching me. They said they would hurt my baby girl." She broke down into sobs.

Maya sat beside her and wrapped an arm around her.

Isabel couldn't believe what she'd heard. That must have been horrifying for Lisa.

"Where did they take you? Where are they holding Aunt Claire? How can we find her?" Isabel asked.

Lisa continued to cry without answering. Isabel softened. "You left us a note. And you brought Daisy home?"

Lisa nodded.

"I just wanted to warn you. I don't even know what's going on. I figured dropping Daisy off would just look like I didn't want her if they were watching me. I just opened the door and let her walk in."

Maya nodded.

"Is Aunt Claire okay?" Maya asked.

"I don't know, sweetie. I really don't know."

———

LISA MADE them sneak out the side door after she checked out the front door a few times. They ran to Andrew's car and drove away while Isabel watched Lisa go back inside and close all the blinds.

Isabel knew Lisa took a big risk helping them. She hoped it never came back to hurt her or her family. Lisa's husband was clearly afraid. This was serious.

"You were right," Sara said. "It is Dr. Rodriguez."

"We have to get into Gennovations. That's definitely where they took them. That's where Aunt Claire and Herbert are. We are back to Plan A," said Isabel.

"What's plan A?"

"We make a delivery, like Andrew said. We are going to have to make it official. I can forge an invoice, and I can probably make some fake ID cards—"

"Um, Isabel," interrupted Andrew. "We actually *do* work there. We can just print an invoice."

"Oh."

Maya chuckled, and they all started laughing. Andrew drove to the feed store and parked in the back. He walked through an employee entrance, and the girls all followed him.

"The good news is that our parents are out of town, so no one will question us until at least Monday."

"Who is working at the store?" said Maya.

"Oh, a bunch of people work here. We have a couple of weekend shifts. I think Candis Johnson is working now. You know her, right, Maya? She's a cheerleader."

Isabel couldn't say for sure, but she thought she saw a flicker of jealousy in Maya's face.

———

ANDREW SAT down at the computer in the office. He showed Maya where they kept uniform shirts, and she sorted through until she found shirts that would fit them all. She put hers on and handed one to Andrew.

"Give me a few minutes, and I'll get everything ready."

Isabel and Sara wandered into the store. Aisle after aisle was filled with all kinds of supplies. In the back, bags of grain and bales of hay were stacked up to the ceiling. Along the wall nearest Isabel hung horse leads and bridles. A few yards away, sample doghouses were lined up on display.

"I am so not in Orange County anymore," said Isabel. Sara laughed.

"Is that where you're from?"

"That's where we lived before, yeah. Aunt Claire moved us here after my parents died."

"I heard about that. I'm sorry about your mom and dad."

"Thank you. Me, too."

"Do you hate it here?"

"Actually, no." She kept walking. "I thought I would, but it's not so bad. I love Aunt Claire, and I really like working with her at the clinic. Plus, I have a lot of opportunity to work on programming—especially since no one here has any decent network security."

"Well, I guess that's good. I kind of hate it."

"You do?"

"Yeah, it's a small town, and people always know everything. Plus, we go to school with the same kids from kindergarten on. And let's just be honest, most of them are jerks."

"That's true."

"When we were little, we were all friends. But now, there are all these cliques, and I'm just not one of the cool kids. So those girls, who've I have known my whole life started picking on me. Well, you saw."

"Yeah. I see that kind of stuff all the time. That's why I don't have any friends."

Sara stopped walking.

"What am I, chopped liver?" she laughed. "I'm your friend."

Isabel hadn't thought about that. "Are you?"

"Of course, I am."

A big smile grew across Isabel's face. "Okay."

Sara laughed.

Maya popped her head through the office door. "Come on, you two. We're ready."

"WE REALLY NEED to get going now," said Andrew. "It will seem suspicious if we get there after five."

"Don't we need some kind of plan?" asked Maya.

"We'll figure out the details on the way," said Andrew. He opened the back door, and they all walked to the delivery van. Andrew began loading pet food into the back.

"We don't really need that, do we," asked Isabel.

"Of course, we need it. They might check the van. Or we might be allowed to unload it into the building. At the very least, we could hide behind it."

"Good thinking," said Maya. The girls began helping Andrew.

Isabel got an idea. "Can I take a few things from the store?"

"Sure, but we need to inventory them first. Sara can help you."

The girls went back in, and Isabel grabbed two bags of treats, several horse leads, and ropes. Isabel listed all the items on a clipboard.

"Why do we need these?"

"We might not, but I figure things like ropes are useful. I don't suppose the feed store carries any kind of GPS?"

"No. But we have maps. Lots of people ride horses on the mountain trails."

"Okay, grab those. Do you have tranquilizers?"

Sara laughed. "No, although after today, I might suggest we start carrying them."

Sara made note of everything they took with them. She and Isabel pulled the uniform shirts on over their clothes. Sara called to Candis, who was working at the front of the store, and told her she and Andrew were going on a delivery for an order that had just come in.

Candis nodded absently and went back to playing with her phone at the counter.

"I THINK Andrew and I should stay up front, and you two should hide in the back," said Maya. "We can say we're making the delivery, and they'll let us through."

"What if they want to search the van, though?" Andrew said. "Considering what they're up to in there and how they treated Officer Williams, I'm sure they will."

"Actually, that gives me an idea," said Isabel. "Before you pull into the gate, Sara and I can hop out. While you're talking to the guards, we'll sneak in behind the guard house on foot. That way, if you guys can't get in, we can. And vice versa."

"I don't like the idea of splitting up," said Andrew.

"We can cover more ground that way," said Sara. "That facility is huge."

Andrew shook his head. He looked in the rearview mirror at Sara.

"No. I don't like it. We need to stick together."

"I agree," said Maya.

"Fine. We'll hide between the bags of food. Hopefully that will work."

"What about once we're inside?" Andrew asked. "Should we just go wherever they send us, then try to look around?"

"Ideally, I need to get to a computer on their network," said Isabel. "Then I might be able to see the security feeds and find Aunt Claire that way."

"That makes sense. Okay, guys, let's get Isabel to a computer. We are just about there—get ready."

Isabel and Sara crouched down together between bags of dog food. Isabel's heart was pounding, and her palms were sweating. She heard Andrew roll down his window and say, "Good afternoon gentleman. I have a delivery."

ELEVEN

Just as they suspected, the guards were on edge.

"Who placed this delivery?"

"We got the call from a 'Mike.'" Andrew responded, looking at the invoice as if he were reading from it.

"We get all of our food from Smith Animal Products," the guard prodded.

"Well, we are having a big sale right now. I guess Mike heard about. And to be honest, we really want your business, so we threw in a few extra pounds of food."

"Open the back," the guard commanded.

Isabel held her breath as she heard Andrew and Maya climb out of the front. They had food stacked all around them, so unless the guards moved it, they would be hidden.

"What's with all the horse stuff? We don't have any horses here."

"Got another delivery after this," said Andrew. "We need to stop by Miller's farm on our way back into town."

He is good on his feet, thought Isabel.

"Alright kid," said the guard, shutting the doors. "Tell Mike he needs to clear this with us next time."

"I'll let him know. Thanks, gentlemen."

Andrew and Maya got back in and began to pull away. Isabel felt Sara let out the breath she'd been holding. She looked over at her.

"We're in. How did you know to say it was Mike?"

"I guessed. I mean every business has a Mike, right? Which way should I go?"

"That sign says loading dock," said Maya. "Let's go this way so we don't have to try to walk through some kind of lobby. You guys couldn't see the gates back there, but we are talking major security."

Andrew turned. He backed the van up to the end of the loading dock. "The fencing is all electric barbed wire, and the gates are like ten feet tall," he added. "It looks like a prison."

"And yet, no one is here," said Isabel, looking around the warehouse through the van windows.

"Because no one is actually expecting a delivery," said Andrew.

Isabel smiled and put on her backpack. She shoved two of the horse leads and the treats into her bag. She and Sara waited for Andrew to open the door, and they all stepped in. The area was a warehouse with tall shelves, filled with pallets. The concrete floor echoed as they stepped, but no one was around to hear.

"Isabel, look." Sara pointed to a small dark office with the door closed and a sign on the door that said WARE-HOUSE MANAGER.

They hurried over. Maya closed the door behind them. Andrew closed the blinds, and Sara turned on the lights.

"The door doesn't lock," Maya said.

"We'll have to keep a lookout," Andrew answered, peeking through the blinds.

It was a tight fit with the four of them in there. Isabel sat in the office chair. The other three looked over her shoulder as the computer turned on. Isabel started typing to interrupt the computer's normal start up process. She bit her lower lip and read the characters as they appeared on the screen.

"Well at least somebody in this town has a legit security system," she said.

Maya looked at her nervously.

"Can you get in?"

"Sure, I can. I'm just saying that it's about time people took their network seriously. Can you grab my laptop out of my backpack?" Isabel never looked away from the screen. When Maya handed her the computer, she turned it on and opened a programing screen. She looked between the two screens as she input characters into the Gennovations computer.

Everyone was tense in the tiny room. Every few minutes, Sara used her fingers to separate the blinds to look out, then turned back to the group to say, "All clear."

"I'm in, guys. Take a look."

Isabel shifted in her seat to allow everyone to see the screen. A number of security cameras showed people walking around different areas, working at their desks, and eating in a break room. She hit a few keys and the cameras rotated through.

"Stop!" Maya cried. "Look at the one in the top right corner."

Isabel selected the screen and zoomed in. It was a laboratory with steel tables and a few stools. A large kennel sat in the corner. Aunt Claire was sitting on the floor next to it. Herbert was inside. They were alone in the room.

"Where is that room?"

The bottom of the screen said BLDGA4. Isabel pulled up the blueprints on her laptop.

"I think that might mean Building A, and 4 is probably the room number."

The blueprints did show a Building A. It was across the campus from where they were now.

"Keep an eye on the security cameras," said Isabel.

"What are you doing?"

"Aunt Claire looks like she is okay right now. I'm going to try to use this time to figure out what information they have."

"I don't think we have time for that," Sara said. "There's someone out there."

Maya gasped.

"He is just sort of strolling around, but I think we should probably hide," Andrew said as he turned the lights back off and they all squeezed under desks and beside filing cabinets. They could hear footsteps coming toward them. Isabel kept her eyes glued to the door handle. She saw it turn and held her breath. The man poked his head in, shined his flashlight around for a second, then stepped back and closed the door again. Isabel exhaled. They waited in their hiding spots as the footsteps faded away.

"That was close," said Maya. "We need to get Aunt Claire and get out of here."

Andrew nodded.

"How are we going to get to Building A?"

"I have a great idea for that," Sara said. "Good thing I have such a strong, athletic big brother."

ISABEL CONTINUED to work on the computer as the others worked on the new plan. Peeking through the blinds, Sara had spotted some blue uniforms in the corner. She slipped out the door and tiptoed to them. Maya went the other direction, looking for a big, empty box. She found one.

Sara brought the uniform to Andrew.

"Put this on. We will sneak out and climb into one of those boxes. You need to get a dolly and wheel the boxes to the right building."

Andrew pulled the uniform over his clothes.

"Someone is coming." Isabel could see a man on one of the security cameras. "Hide!"

"Maya is still out there," said Isabel.

"Hide." Andrew commanded. He rushed toward Maya and motioned for her to get in the box. Isabel and Sara ducked under the desk in the office and listened.

"Hey! What are you doing in here?"

"Hello there. I'm just bringing some supplies over to Building A."

"Oh. Alright. I'll give you a hand."

Isabel and Sara looked at each other with wide eyes.

"Uh... thanks but that's okay. I was just about to get a dolly."

"I'll grab it."

"Thanks."

Isabel and Sara could hear whispering but couldn't make out the words.

"Here we go," said the man. "Just tip the box and I'll slide the dolly underneath."

Isabel heard some movement and the squeak of the dolly wheels.

"I'm actually headed over to Building A too. I'll walk with you."

"Uh, thank you very much for your help."

"No problem, man. Come on."

Their footsteps faded away.

"I guess we split up after all," said Sara.

SARA STARTED PACING around the small office, running her fingers through her short, smooth hair.

"Sara, calm down. Look."

Isabel was sitting at the computer desk again, using the security camera footage to follow Andrew's movements out of the building. After a few minutes, Andrew appeared on a screen that said BLDGA1 on the bottom. The other man patted him on the back and headed down a hallway. Andrew looked up and down the hallway, then spoke into the box. He started down the hallway again, peeking in windows as he went.

"He's going to find Aunt Claire. He's sticking to the plan, just without us. This is kind of perfect because they can look around and we can mine the data."

Sara's eyes were glued to the screen. Isabel could feel her shallow breathing against her hair.

"You keep an eye on them," Isabel said, turning back to her own laptop. If she had to stay here, she could try to keep digging.

A few minutes later, Sara tapped her on the shoulder. Isabel turned to the security footage. Andrew was walking down an empty hallway, but outside one of the doors stood a security guard. He was blocking the window and barricading the door. It was hard to tell in the security video, but it looked like a padlock hung on the door.

"Aunt Claire is probably in that room," said Isabel.

Just then, the door to the office swung open. "What are you kids doing in here?" A man barked. He grabbed his radio and shouted into it.

"Run, Isabel!" Sara shouted, as she grabbed Isabel's arm and pulled her. The girls ran on either side of the man, confusing him. They hurried down the aisles, zigging and zagging around. The man chased them and yelled at them to stop. Isabel saw an exit and sprinted for it. She pushed it open and dove outside. She tripped over a rock and rolled down a hill. Sara was running down the hill behind her. The man wasn't yelling anymore.

Isabel stopped rolling and landed on her back. She jumped up, just as Sara reached the bottom of the small hill. They dashed toward another building. As they scooted around the building, Isabel looked over her shoulder. The man was not behind them.

A small staircase lead to a door. They hid behind the stairs and tried to catch their breath.

"I think we outran him, but the whole security team is going to be looking for us now," said Isabel, through heavy breaths. "I left my laptop back there."

It was starting to get dark outside. The cold air was nipping at Isabel's sweaty skin and giving her chills. She could see her breath leaving her mouth in short, fast spurts. She could hear people moving around nearby, yelling to each other. They were getting closer.

"What are we going to do?" Sara's eyes were wet with tears and her hands were shaking.

"We have to move, but we have to do it slowly. We need a better place to hide."

Isabel stood up with her back against the wall and stepped sideways along the building. Sara followed her lead. When she reached the corner, Isabel peeked around it.

A man was heading right toward them. She pushed on Sara, and they moved the other direction. Sara looked around the corner.

"There are people coming," she said. "They're coming, Isabel. They're going to find us."

Suddenly, they heard a car honking and the sound of an engine. They looked up to see the delivery van driving wildly around on the path between two buildings, spewing up dirt and rocks behind it. A group of security guards were chasing them in a golf cart.

Isabel jumped out from behind the building. She stood on the path and started waving her arms frantically. "ANDREW! MAYA! OVER HERE!"

Maya, who was sitting in the passenger seat, saw her and pointed to her. Andrew drove the van toward them. He barely paused long enough for Isabel and Sara to jump in. Then he sped off again, fishtailing the back end of the van. Sara grabbed onto the seats to keep herself still, while Isabel was tossed around and landed on the floor of the van, tangled up in ropes and bridles. A bag of dog food slid toward her, and she stuck out her foot to stop it.

Andrew drove off the road, making a beeline for the guard house. The exit gate was closing. Andrew sped up. Guards stood in front of the van but dove out of the way as Andrew continued to speed toward the gate. The gate slammed into the side the van and scraped down the side of it as they drove through. The windows shattered, but Andrew kept going. He sped out onto the road, then turned onto the main highway, speeding toward the safety of town.

"WHAT HAPPENED?" Maya asked.

"We were watching you on the camera when someone came in and saw us," Sara answered. "We ran for it. We were hiding behind that building when we heard the van. How did you know we were caught?"

"It was impossible not to know. The whole place went on lockdown and there were alarms going off everywhere. We saw a man run by screaming at someone to find you. We were just trying to distract them with the van so you could get away when we saw you waving your arms."

"That's insane," said Sara. "Thanks for saving us, guys."

Isabel knew she should say something like that, but she didn't. She just looked down at the floor of the van.

"I have good news and bad news," said Isabel. "The bad news is, I left my laptop there. Any data I could have gotten is gone, and I've got no way to get back in. The good news is I have remote access on my laptop."

"What does that mean," asked Sara.

"It means I can access my laptop from another computer. I can log in and it would be just like I was sitting in front of it. There are two problems though: I can only do it if my laptop is turned on, and while I'm doing it, the screen will show all of my movements. So, if I open a file remotely, it will open on that laptop screen too."

Sara nodded. "So, it's risky. Can they track where the other computer is?"

"No, but if they know what I'm doing, they'll destroy the computer immediately."

"That's all very interesting," said Maya. "But we have a pretty long list of other problems, too, starting with the fact that they are looking for us, they know where we live, and they know where this delivery van is from."

"We have to go back to the police," said Andrew. "I can only imagine how glad they'll be to see us this time."

TWELVE

Andrew parked the van in the front of the police station. The front end was smashed in, and the windshield was cracked all the way across. The gate had left giant ugly scrapes along both sides. One of the fenders was half hanging off.

"Mom and Dad are going to kill me," he said, running his hands through his hair and shaking his head. Sara patted him on the arm.

When they walked into the station, the dispatcher at the front jumped up and yelled for Officer Williams. Officer Williams slammed the door open and stared at them.

"You kids are killing me. Get in here." The look on his face was a mixture of anger and relief. He led them into a small conference room with eight old but cushy chairs around a table.

"Somebody better start talking right now," he demanded. "I want to know everything."

Isabel hesitated. She did not want to tell him about Lisa.

She started the story herself, and she told him every single thing except that. She hoped the others figured it out.

Officer Williams stared at her, his mouth hanging open.

"You realize how dangerous this all was, right? And that a lot of it is illegal? Especially the part where you tricked one of my officers?" Officer Williams stood up. He was pacing all around the room now.

"We had no choice. Your hands were tied. Ours weren't," said Isabel.

"You very well may have made things worse. You are not the police. You are kids."

"With all due respect, Officer," said Maya. "I think we are focused on all the wrong things here."

Officer Williams looked dumbstruck.

"We should be focused on the fact that Aunt Claire is, for sure, being held against her will in a room inside the Gennovations facility. In fact, she is being held in Room 4 of Building A."

"Actually, I might even be able to show you," said Isabel.

ISABEL WAS SITTING at a cubicle in the police station. It took a while, but she was able to get the software she needed and was logged in. She took a deep breath and whispered, "Please work."

She clicked *connect*.

A moment later the computer screen blinked. When it came back, it was her laptop screen. Everyone cheered. Maya and Andrew even high-fived. Isabel bit her bottom lip and worked her way through the necessary applications to access the security cameras again. She pulled up Room 4 camera, but the room was empty.

"She's not there," said Sara.

The four of them stared in the screen in disbelief.

"They must have moved her after we left," said Andrew. "That makes sense, actually. But where did they move her to?"

Isabel scrolled through the cameras, one by one, but they could not see Aunt Claire anywhere. She went back to Room 4.

"Herbert is still there," she said. "See him? He's sleeping in the kennel."

"Isn't that enough," Maya said to Officer Williams. "Can't you get a warrant or something now?"

Officer Williams covered his mouth with his hand. "I'm not exactly sure this is legal. Hacking into their system like this. While I personally don't mind, I don't know that I can find a judge who'd sign a warrant based on this."

Suddenly, the screen blinked again, and a text box opened. The cursor started blinking and then someone started typing.

Hi Isabel. You sure are good at this.

Everyone stared at the screen. Isabel felt her heart beat all the way in her throat.

I am giving you this one and only warning. Stop this or you will regret it.

The screen blinked again and then when black.

Isabel's stomach churned. She felt sweat forming at her hairline.

"This is bad," said Maya. "These are bad people. They know where we are. They know how to find us, all of us. And they have Aunt Claire."

"THIS IS what I've been trying to tell you kids," Officer Williams said, finally softening. "This is why I didn't want you running off and why I assigned an officer to stay with you. This is dangerous."

"If anyone is in danger, it's Aunt Claire!" shouted Isabel. "We are fine. We are all standing here, fine. Aunt Claire is trapped in a locked room with those people. We have to save her. We have to go right now."

Isabel was crying. Tears were streaming down her face, and she hiccupped. Sara moved over and put her arm around her.

"This is a police matter," said Officer Williams. "We will handle it. What you kids need to do is listen to me and follow my directions. You will not leave this station again."

Maya nodded. They walked back into the conference room and sat around the table. Officer Williams told them he would order a pizza for them, and he left the room.

Isabel put her head in her hands and tried to think. *Where did they move Aunt Claire? Was she okay? Could the police save her?*

"The good news is," Sara spoke up, interrupting her thoughts as if she heard them, "they won't hurt Claire. They can't. They need her, right? I mean, they need her brilliant mind."

"But what if she refuses to help them?" Andrew asked.

"I'm sure that's what happening," Maya said. "There is no way Aunt Claire would give them what they want. She knows they have bad intentions for this research. She wants to help people with disabilities; Gennovations wants to make amped-up guard dogs and who knows what else. She will never help them."

"Do you think they've realized that yet?' asked Andrew.

AS ISABEL SAT in the conference room eating pizza, she thought of her mom. She knew how stubborn Aunt Claire was, and how virtuous and strong she would be to protect what she thought was right. She knew because Mom was just the same.

Isabel wiped a tear from her cheek, hoping no one saw it. She wished her parents were there. She wished they could help. She wished she could talk to them. She got up and went to the restroom to splash water on her face. She leaned against the sink, taking deep breaths, and letting the water drip off her skin.

She heard someone yelling, and she jumped. Sirens went off outside. Isabel ran out of the bathroom back to the conference room in time to see her friends run out looking afraid and confused.

Officer Williams ran down the hall.

"Gonzalez, stay with the kids. Ugh. Where is that social worker? Kids, you need to stay here and listen to the officer. Do you hear me?"

They all nodded as Officer Williams ran out the door.

"What's going on?" Isabel demanded.

"I have no idea," said Sara. "But it must be bad."

They looked out the window as every single police cruiser sped away with their sirens wailing and their lights flashing.

ISABEL STOMPED up to Officer Gonzalez and leaned forward. She wasn't even shoulder height to him, but she stood her ground, looking up.

"Tell us what is going on."

"I don't know if I can. I just need you to stay here and stay calm. Can I get you anything?"

"No, you can't get us anything. You can tell us what the heck is happening!"

The officer looking nervously over at the dispatcher, who was standing in the doorway, still wearing her telephone headset. She shrugged her shoulders.

"I would tell them. They'll find out in a few minutes anyway."

Officer Gonzalez sighed.

"Okay, but listen to me. You must promise me, if I tell you, you won't do anything stupid. If I tell you, you will all march yourselves back into that conference room and wait patiently until we get some news."

Despite herself, Isabel was a little bit proud of how nervous they all made the officers.

"Okay, of course," said Maya. "We will stay, but what's happening? Is it Aunt Claire?"

The dispatcher nodded encouragingly at Gonzalez.

"We got a call," he started, then paused and took a deep breath. "We got a call from a man claiming to be holding Claire hostage at a warehouse outside of town. He put Claire on the phone for a few seconds, so we know she is with him. All units are responding right now."

Maya covered her mouth with her hand and mumbled something to herself.

"What warehouse?" asked Isabel, with a note of skepticism in her voice.

"An old, abandoned warehouse on the south edge of the city."

Something about that seemed very wrong to Isabel. She knew Aunt Claire was at the Gennovations facility. Why would someone take her all the way to the other end of the city? And why an abandoned warehouse when they had that entire locked-down Gennovations campus to hold her that the police couldn't enter?

Something was wrong. She could feel it in her gut.

THEY ALL WENT BACK into the conference room, but no one sat down. Maya chewed on her bottom lip. She crossed her arms protectively around herself and kept whispering. Isabel thought she might be praying.

Isabel, on the other hand, was pacing like a caged animal. She gnawed on her fingernails. Despite the chilly fall air, she was sweating.

It seemed like they had been waiting for hours, though the clock told her it had been under five minutes. That's when she heard the bang.

Officer Gonzalez yelled something, and the dispatcher screamed. Isabel bolted out of the room just in time to see Officer Gonzalez hit the floor and twitch, taser lines connected to his shoulders. Five huge men wearing all black had stormed in. The dispatcher was laying on the floor, too.

"It's a trap! It's a trap!" Officer Williams yelled over the radio, seconds too late. "Get those kids out of there!"

The man in the front of the group looked up and saw Isabel.

"Run!" she screamed and bolted down the hallway. As she came around the corner, another man stepped in her way and wrapped his arms around her. She kicked and screamed. She tried to scratch him and elbow him, but she was completely overpowered by his size. She saw Maya running outside; she was strong and fast, her legs and arms pumping. Out of nowhere, a man came at her and took her down. They both tumbled to the ground. Maya hit and kicked at him and landed a few hard blows. Another man ran up to help him, and together they held Maya. They flipped her onto her stomach and put zip ties around her wrists behind her back.

Isabel squirmed in the man's arms, pushing him, and kicking against the walls. Soon, another man ran up and grabbed both of her ankles. He zip-tied them before they laid her on the ground and tied her wrists.

She spat out every dirty word and insult she could at them, but they ignored her. One of the men lifted her up over his shoulder and carried her back down the hallway as if she were a petulant child being put in timeout.

"You'll never get away with this. This is a police station. You assaulted officers, and there are cameras everywhere." She squirmed and kicked, but the man had no trouble holding her.

Outside, he opened the back door to the gray van, swung her off his shoulder, and placed her inside. When she looked up, she was glad to see that his lip was bleeding, and he had a growing bruise on his cheek. He reached for her pocket and grabbed her phone from it.

She kicked at him, and he slammed the door.

It was entirely dark inside the van, but Isabel could hear the breathing and whimpering of others.

"Who's in here? Maya, is that you?"

"It's all three of us," said Andrew. "Are you guys all okay?"

"A little scratched but okay," said Maya. "Are everyone's hands and feet zip tied?"

"Mine are," Sara confirmed. "I'm sorry guys, I didn't put

up much of a fight. I was too scared." Her voice cracked, and she sniffled a few times.

"That's okay Sara," Andrew said. "It was scary."

"Isabel and Maya put up a big fight. You guys gave them hell."

"A lot of good it did us," said Maya. "I've never been tackled by an enormous bad guy before."

"You took it well," said Andrew. "Maybe you should start playing football."

No one laughed at the joke. Isabel knew exactly where they were going, but she had no idea what to expect once they got there.

THIRTEEN

When they arrived at Gennovations, they were immediately waved through the gate. Isabel couldn't see anything outside the van, but by the number of voices she heard, it sounded like they had added a lot of guards. After a short drive, the van stopped, and the engine was turned off.

Isabel was ready to fight when the doors opened again. As soon as a man reached in, she kicked out both feet, hitting him in the stomach. She squirmed and yelled, kicking and flailing about. Someone grabbed her by the ankles and pulled her from the van, dropping her hard against the ground. She could taste blood in her mouth as she lifted her head up.

"Stop fighting us, little girl. Even if you got away, there's nowhere to run. Now knock it off before we taser you, too."

She knew he was right, but she had no intention of making their jobs any easier. The men pulled all four of them inside a building and locked the door behind them. A man spoke into his radio.

"All doors secured?"

"10-4," the radio sounded back.

"Okay, cut their feet so they can walk," he told the others. "They can't get out of the building."

A man cut the zip tie around Isabel's ankles. She tried to kick him, but he moved too fast. He grabbed her roughly by one arm and yanked her to her feet. Another man pulled out his taser and held it in his hand. He stared at her and cocked one eyebrow, as if daring her to keep it up.

The men led them down a narrow hallway into a big empty room. The lights were off, but the light coming in from the hallway shined in. There were no tables or chairs, just empty white space, and a big window on one side. They sat the kids against the opposite wall, turned and walked out, slamming the door, and leaving them in the dark. Isabel heard the lock click into place.

"What are they going to do with us?" Sara asked.

"I don't know," said Andrew. "I can't figure out if they need us for something or if they just wanted us out of the way. Maybe they just brought us in here so we would stop asking questions and stop feeding information to the police."

Isabel doubted that, though it sounded good. She hoped it gave Sara a little bit of comfort.

UNFORTUNATELY, it did not take long for Isabel to find out. The lights in the room came on suddenly. The brightness stung Isabel's eyes, and she blinked rapidly to get them to adjust. Dr. Rodriguez walked in.

"Welcome to Gennovations, kids. We are so glad you're here."

Isabel jumped up and tried to run at him, but he dodged

her, and she stumbled. The light had disoriented her, and she was less agile with her arms secured behind her. She tripped and fell forward. Without her arms to catch herself, she hit her face on the ground. When she sat up, blood was tricking down her face from her nose.

"Whoa. Whoa. Settle down, or I'll have to have Bruce tie up your legs again." He nodded toward the window and a moment later the big security guard who held Isabel down earlier walked in. He stood next to the door with his arms across his chest.

"Honestly, I do wish we wouldn't have had to bring you in here. I really do. Especially you two." He motioned at Andrew and Sara. Sara was huddled against her big brother. "You're not useful to me at all, but unfortunately, you all stuck together and then stuck your nose where it didn't belong so... here we all are." He spread out his arms wide. "And now you're going to help me."

"We will never help you!" screamed Isabel. "Where is Aunt Claire? What are you doing to her?" As she yelled, blood that had dripped down into her mouth spewed out at him. He stepped backward and made a face.

"Oh, don't worry, she's fine. The problem is that she's been extremely uncooperative. Now I've tried to be nice, I even offered her a job. I'm sure you girls remember—you were sitting under the window, after all. I tried to convince her to work with me. There are millions of dollars to be made here. I would have shared it with her. But I most certainly will not compete with her for it. I'm smarter than that." A sly smile appeared on his cruel face as he tapped his index finger against his temple. "You are all going to help me convince Claire to cooperate. We are all going to work together."

"We would never help you," Isabel spat.

"I'm sure you will find me very, very persuasive. But before we get started, which one of you is the hacker?"

No one answered Dr. Rodriguez, but it didn't matter. Bruce knew. He'd done his homework on the girls.

"Of course, it's the feisty one," Dr. Rodriguez sighed. "Okay, better bring her with us."

"No!" screamed Maya. "It's not her, it's me. I'm the hacker."

Isabel's throat tightened. She thought of all the mean, cruel things she'd said to Maya, but Maya still tried to sacrifice herself to protect her. Isabel stared at her sister and blinked back tears. Dr. Rodriguez looked at Bruce. He shook his head.

"It's the younger one," Bruce said. "This one is the athlete."

"Let's go," Dr. Rodriguez said.

Bruce walked over and grabbed Isabel by the arm. Maya and Sara started screaming. Andrew stood up and tried to get in between them, but Bruce just shoved him to the ground with one hand. Isabel nearly fell over as Bruce dragged her from the room. She was dizzy, but she could hear the others screaming for her.

"She's going to be difficult," said Bruce. "We might have more luck with the doctor if we bring the other niece in with her."

Isabel could vaguely make that out.

"Take me! Take me to Aunt Claire! Where is she?"

"You have other work to do," said Bruce. "Our network guy has a whole lot of questions for you."

"That's too bad. I'm not doing anything to help you or your network guy. Take me to Aunt Claire."

They pulled her down the hallway and she stumbled, trying keep up. Bruce yanked her from place to place. They went down a hallway, then turned and hurried down another hallway, then turned again. Isabel completely lost her sense of direction. He pushed open some swinging doors and pulled her through, then made another sharp turn and opened a door into a large room. Computer screens glared at her from every direction, but only one person sat in the room.

"Is this her?" said a tall man. He was sitting at his computer screen and had not looked at them yet. He wore slacks and a button-down shirt and had on trendy glasses. He certainly didn't look like a security guard, or a doctor for that matter.

"I'm Greg. I'm the head of the information systems department and you've been a real pain in my side," he said with a tinge of humor in his voice. "Although, I must admit, I'm pretty impressed. How old are you?"

She glared at him, blood still trickling down her face. Finally, he turned his head and looked at her. His mouth dropped open, and his eyes widened.

"What did you do to her Bruce?"

"I convinced her to help you. Where do you want her?"

Greg was visibly worried. He looked up at Bruce, then swallowed hard. "Um, over here is fine." He motioned toward an empty workstation. Bruce shoved her into the chair.

"She's certainly not going to be able to do anything with her hands tied behind her back."

"Trust me, Greg, you want her restrained."

"She can't be restrained and do what I need her to do, Bruce."

"Suit yourself," Bruce said. "But don't say I didn't warn you."

Bruce cut the zip ties off Isabel. She shook out her arms

and rubbed her wrists with her hands. Bruce went over to the door and stood in front of it, with his arms crossed. Isabel rolled her eyes at him.

"You don't scare me," she said. Then she turned to Greg. "I'm not going to help you do anything."

Greg looked at Bruce. Bruce nodded.

"I'm not really sure what the circumstances are here," said Greg. "But I need you to un-code this encrypted data. We can't seem to break your system. And then I need you to show me how you hacked into our security feed."

"No," she said. "I've already told you. I won't help. And the police are probably on their way, so I think you should all think twice about what you're doing right now."

"Bruce, what are we doing right now? Why are the police coming?"

Bruce walked over to Isabel. He leaned down close to her face. She could feel his hot breath on her skin. Their noses were almost touching.

"You're going to do what we ask," he said. "You'll do it now, or I'll find another way to convince you. Keep in mind, all the people you love are currently in my custody."

Isabel's face dropped. Fear drained the resistance from her.

"You will do what we ask, or I'll drag your sister in here and I'll change your mind."

Isabel looked at Greg. He looked horrified.

"Bruce... I... What's going on?"

"Get the data, Greg. Dr. Rodriguez needs it."

"Can you log me into your system, please?" Isabel asked meekly. "That will save us some time."

Greg was nervous. Isabel could tell how uncomfortable this situation was making him. He might be her best chance.

"Do you have my laptop? I can show you how I remoted in."

Greg retrieved Isabel's entire backpack. She saw they'd stuffed her laptop back into its padded spot at some point. She pulled out the computer.

The room was silent except for the hum of the computer towers. The men were watching Isabel very carefully.

She opened a screen that showed the code on the back end of her system. She scrolled through it to find the encoding commands.

Greg kept wringing his hands, looking from Isabel to Bruce.

"Here it is," she pointed to it on the screen.

"We found that," Greg replied. "But we couldn't disable it."

Isabel nodded. That had been her intent, but she was stalling, hopeful that if she gave them something, it might look like she was cooperating.

Just then, Bruce's radio sounded.

"Bruce! Get back here! We have a situation!"

"I can't leave the girl," he said.

"We need you here now."

He looked over at Greg and Isabel.

"We're okay here," said Greg. "She's helping."

"I don't trust her as far as I can throw her. I'm locking you both in here. If you give Greg any trouble, you will pay for it."

Isabel nodded.

"Bruce! Help!" his radio shouted again.

He hurried out of the door and locked it.

"What's going on here? Are you being held against your will?" Greg asked breathlessly.

As quickly as she could, Isabel explained to Greg what was going on. His eyes were wide, and he covered his hand with his mouth.

"I need your help, Greg, but if you help me, they might hurt you. We have to make it look like you didn't."

Isabel explained her plan. She would fix the encoded data, but then encode it again, in a different, more subtle way. When Dr. Rodriquez looked at it, it would seem to make sense, but when he read it closely, it would just be Wikipedia articles on genetic modification.

"Are the police really on their way," he asked.

"I don't know. They kidnapped us from the police station, but I don't know how many officers have been hurt or how many know where we are."

Greg nodded and told her to do it.

"Keep working, I'm going to call 911. If you see Bruce coming, scream."

Isabel finished working on her code, just as Greg returned.

"I got through; they already knew you were here."

Isabel nodded.

"Now I have a plan," he said. "I'm going to unlock that door for you. I can do it remotely, but I need you to make it look like you escaped. Find something you can use to tie me to the chair."

She reached into her backpack and pulled out the horse leads. She held them up to Greg.

"Perfect," he said. He sat still while Isabel restrained him. Then he told her how to open the door. "One more thing, Isabel. I need you to hit me."

"I don't want to."

"I understand, but for my sake, it needs to look like I tried to stop you. It's for my protection."

She was so grateful to Greg for his help. He had risked a lot, and she could only imagine what Bruce would do if he found out.

With tears gathering in the corners or her eyes, she pulled her arm back and punched him. Her knuckles stung like crazy from the impact. She'd given him a bloody nose. It looked pretty bad, as she supposed he would want.

"Now take my ID that is sitting on the desk, get out of here, and find a place to hide until the cops get here." He smiled at her as best he could through the pain. "Good luck, Isabel."

"Thank you, Greg. I'll never forget this," she said, throwing her backpack over her shoulder.

"If you ever want a job, look me up," he smiled.

Isabel turned and walked to the door.

ISABEL STUCK her head into the hallway and looked around. No one was coming. She couldn't remember where they'd come from or where the others were, so she just turned left and right a few times to try to throw Bruce off her trail when he eventually came looking for her. She knew she was getting lost in the halls, but it was a risk she'd have to take to stay hidden. A sudden sound startled her, and then she heard footsteps in the distance.

She sidestepped down the hall with her back against the wall, like a spy. She listened carefully and ducked into bathrooms or hallways when she thought she heard someone coming. After a few turns this way and that, she turned a corner into a long hallway. There were heavy, solid double doors at the end and a sign that said LABORATORY – RESTRICTED ACCESS. When she got closer, she could see it was dark inside the room, so this wasn't the lab where they were holding Aunt Claire. She heard someone coming. She tried the doors, but they were locked. The footsteps were getting closer. She pulled Greg's ID from her pocket and waved it in front of a sensor on the wall. It beeped, a green light flashed, and she scampered inside, pulling the door closed behind her.

She sat on the floor in the dark with her back against a steel table, trying to catch her breath. That's when she heard a low, fierce growl. She looked around in the dark but couldn't see. The growl came again from her left, a few feet away. She scurried backwards away from it.

When her foot hit something behind her, she reached her hand back to feel what she ran into without looking away from the source of the growl. Her fingers touched cold metal. She dragged her fingers along and realized it was narrow little poles, the kind that make up the front of a kennel. She must be in a lab with animals.

She felt calmer knowing that the animals were in kennels, so whatever had growled at her was probably locked up. She desperately wanted to turn on the lights, but she didn't know if there were any windows in this room. She might give herself away. She stood up and walked around, trying to get a sense of the room. She traced her fingertips carefully along walls and furnishings as she walked, arms outstretched. She could feel the kennel bars on her left and the smooth countertop on her right. She made her way slowly forward, her footsteps squeaking on the linoleum floor. The countertop edge turned to a corner, so she followed it right and continued creeping along. Again, she felt a corner and turned. By now, she could hear an array of animal sounds, sniffing and moving around, claws clicking against the kennel floors. She reached the last corner and saw something glowing in the back corner of a kennel. It looked like a pattern, but it was all curled up on itself, and she could not make it out. When she was satisfied the walls were all lined with kennels and not windows, she approached the doors and felt around for a light switch. When she found it and turned it on, she had to close her eyes from the brightness. When her eyes adjusted, she looked around and could not believe what she saw.

FOURTEEN

Isabel's eyes were wide as she stepped slowly around the room in the light. She stopped at the place where she'd seen something glow. A snake lay coiled up in the back corner, looking at her, sticking its tongue out.

"You glow in the dark," she said, as if the snake knew what that meant.

She looked at the next kennel, where the growl came from. A huge brown dog, bigger than she'd ever seen, stared back at her, teeth bared. His muscle definition was exaggerated like a body builder.

"It's okay," she said. "I won't hurt you."

She moved closer to him and realized his eyes did not follow. She moved slowly so as not to startle him, and she talked in a gentle voice.

"Do they hurt you here, buddy? Are you okay?" Her voice seemed to soothe him. The closer she got, the more she could see that they did. His muscles were so large he moved awkwardly, unsure where he fit. She stepped in front of the kennel, and he seemed to look past her.

"Are you blind? Can you see me?" She waved her hand in front of him, but he did not respond.

She stood up again and walked around. Each kennel housed an animal. Some looked perfectly normal, like perhaps they had not been experimented on. Others were obvious test cases.

Along the back, she saw a cat with enormous paws. When she approached, it hissed at her, and the fur on its back stood up. She spoke to the cat in a soothing voice, but it did not relax. She had an idea—she remembered the treats she took from the feed store.

She opened her backpack and pulled out the treats. She slipped one into the kennel. The cat stayed back.

"I'll just leave that there for you," she said. Then she walked back over to the dog and offered him a treat through the bars. He sniffed at her then licked it up. He gently wagged his tail, though it seemed painful for him.

Isabel opened the kennel a little and reached her hand inside. She let the dog smell her hand. She opened it a little further and petted his head. She gave him another treat. Finally, she took a deep breath and opened the kennel all the way. The dog stepped toward her face. She held her breath. Seconds ticked by. Then the dog licked her face.

She petted him all over and scratched him behind his ears.

Then, she heard a scream.

ISABEL JUMPED BACKWARDS. She couldn't tell who had screamed. She needed to get back to her family, but she didn't know where they were. She'd have to find them without getting caught. She looked around.

"Will you guys help me?" she asked the animals. "I just need you to create a distraction."

She ran around the room, starting with the seemingly normal animals and opened their kennels. They rushed out and began running around the room. Dogs chased each other. Cats jumped on top of the cabinets and counters. Birds flew in circles around the room. Isabel stood back and watched for a minute. She giggled for a second before realizing she'd better hurry.

"Here we go." She rushed toward the big double doors and pushed them open. Animals fled from the room in every direction. She went back to the cat with the huge paws.

"Do you want out?" She reached for the kennel latch. The cat stepped forward. Isabel gently swung the door open and stepped back.

The cat leaped from the kennel onto the floor. Despite its huge paws, it walked normally, smoothly. As it strode out the double doors, it turned back and looked at her one last time.

A moment later, she heard someone running through the halls. She could hear shouts coming toward her.

She grabbed her backpack and opened a cabinet, slipping inside. Footsteps came running in. A voice called out.

"Every kennel's open and empty. The girl must have let the experiment animals out and run for it. The room is empty."

The response was harder to hear. Isabel thought he must have been talking into his radio. She thought she heard a command for everyone to find her. She held her breath. Footsteps echoed through the room. Slowly, the person moved closer.

She heard a cabinet door open and close. The realization that he was looking for her took her breath away. Her whole body started shaking. Another cabinet opened and closed. The person stepped around the next corner, away from her.

Thinking this might be her only chance, she quickly opened the cabinet door and slipped out, leaving her backpack behind. Staying crouched down, she scooted on her knees toward the double doors. When she looked up, she was face to face with the angry cat—their noses almost touching, their eyes locked on each other's. Before Isabel could move, a man came around the corner.

"Hey! Stop right there!" Isabel and the cat both looked up at him. The cat looked back at Isabel and meowed loudly. Suddenly the cat pounced at the man. He stepped backwards and stumbled. Seeing her chance, Isabel ran from the room.

ISABEL RAN AS FAST as she could without looking where she was going. She saw an exit sign and headed for it. She used Greg's ID to open it. When she emerged outside, it was extremely dark and eerily quiet. She tried to orient herself. She'd been here before. She'd run around outside. Where was she?

Why is it so quiet out here? she thought. She'd expected to see security guards running around everywhere. She looked all around at the other buildings. They all looked deserted; no lights were on in any of them. Everything must be happening in Building A. She spotted the warehouse, where she'd sneaked in the first time. It was far away, across a lot of open land. Still, she felt like that'd be the best place to try to access the network again. Isabel took a deep breath and ran as fast as she could. When she looked to her left, she saw the guard house. There were people everywhere, but they were all looking out. Waiting for the police, she thought.

She reached the building, breathless and scared, and yanked on the door. It was locked. Of course. She tried Greg's ID and it didn't work. Either they figured out that she had it or Greg didn't have warehouse access.

She went around the back of the building where they'd parked the van last time. One of the roll-up doors was open just a bit. She laid down on her stomach and squeezed herself underneath it. She ran through the dark aisles of the warehouse and into the small office in the corner, closing the door behind her.

With the lights off, she crawled under the desk and took deep breaths, hoping no one followed. She listened for footsteps for a long time before getting up the courage to climb into the office chair and power on the computer on the desk. It took merely seconds for her to pull up the security feed. This time, Isabel decided to record her screen as she worked. She scrolled through empty room after empty room. She saw Greg in his office. He was untied now and was focused on the screen in front of him. Finally, she found the big empty room, where they had been held before. Tears streamed down her face instantly.

Maya and Sara were gone. As were the guards. Andrew lay on the floor, facedown. She stared at the screen for a long time, willing him to get up or move around, something to show her that he was okay. He lay still.

I must keep looking, she thought, taking a deep breath. She finally spotted Sara. She was in the same room where Aunt Claire had been held before. She was sitting on the floor next to the kennel. She had reached inside and was petting Herbert. Though the video quality wasn't great, it looked like Sara was okay. She couldn't see any obvious injuries anywhere, and she was sitting up.

Isabel leaned back against the desk. What had they done? They should never have told Andrew and Sara what was going on. They never should have asked them for help. This was her fault. *She* had told Maya to call Andrew the first time they left the police station. *She* got them into this mess.

It was always her fault. Maya had been right. If she hadn't gotten in trouble at school, Mom and Dad would never have been on that road at that time. They would have been at work, safe from the dangers of the road. It was her fault they were all here now. If she never would have encoded the data, Dr. Rodriguez would have gotten it the first time he broke into the lab. He would have had what he needed and would never have come back for Aunt Claire. If it wasn't for her, everyone would be okay.

She wiped her tears and continued scrolling through security feeds.

She finally found Aunt Claire. She was in a room with a bunch of people. It looked like a combination of security guards and researchers. They were all looking at Aunt Claire. She was sitting on a stool with her arms crossed. She wasn't speaking or looking at any of them. Dr. Rodriguez was there, too. He seemed to be talking.

Suddenly, a door burst open in that room, and a big man dragged Maya through it. Aunt Claire jumped up and tried to go to Maya, but security guards restrained her. Maya reached out to Aunt Claire, too. They held her back. Dr. Rodriguez stepped in between them and said something to Aunt Claire. She stopped fighting. Her shoulders sagged, and she nodded, while looking at the floor.

A man ran into the room and said something that made all the security guards look up in alarm. They must have realized Isabel had escaped again. She could vaguely see a smile creep on Maya's face. Dr. Rodriguez pounded his fist on the table and yelled something. Several guards ran from the room.

Isabel knew they'd be looking for her. She made sure the connection was still working but turned off the monitor. She pulled her knees in under the desk and pulled the chair into the tiny space with her. Fortunately, her small stature allowed her to tuck the chair all the way in. It concealed her completely. Then she waited.

IT ONLY TOOK a few minutes for someone to come looking. She heard a door open and saw lights turn on through the blinds of the office window. The office door swung open, and footsteps entered the room. She held her breath. The seconds took hours as two sets of feet made their way into the room. They peeked around the desk but did not move the chair.

"Clear," said one man. The two quickly left the room.

Isabel waited for a long time. The door was left open, and she could hear sounds outside as the guards searched the warehouse. Her only option was to stay still until they moved on.

But then what? Isabel tried to think of a plan. How could she get to the others without being seen? Were the police on their way or would they be stuck at the guard gate? At the very least, she hoped that being missing was creating a distraction that might help Aunt Claire and Maya. She knew if she went anywhere near them, she'd be met by more guards. She also imagined Bruce was probably pretty unhappy with her right now. She didn't know what he might do to her, and she had not seen him on the security footage.

Don't panic, she told herself. *Think this through.*

She took a few deep breaths before climbing back into the office chair and turning the monitor back on, praying no one was in the warehouse to see the light. If Greg could access the door locks through their system, surely, she could access a few other things.

She hacked into the network system again. This time all the firewalls were down. She wondered if Greg had done that, letting her in on purpose, knowing she might try it. She started to poke around, and when she found the central control, a big smile grew on her face. She clicked a button and watched as the power went down all around her.

FIFTEEN

First, she wanted to create a little chaos. She killed the power in the main buildings. She locked the door to the warehouse and rolled down the open door.

Then, she unlocked every door she could access within the main building. She watched as Sara realized it. Sara stood up and bolted from the room, running for her brother. Isabel turned on lights to guide her way, then shut them back off behind her, and Sara followed. When Isabel saw Sara reach Andrew, she pressed her lips together and clenched her firsts.

"Please, please, please," she said. Sara reached down and touched Andrew. A few seconds later, he stirred. Relief overwhelmed her. Silent tears slid down her cheeks.

She switched back to the room with Aunt Claire and Maya. She couldn't see much in that dark room. She turned on the lights and saw the room was empty. She could see flashlight beams coming from the hallway. She changed views again. She turned on the lights in the hallway. Four guards had Aunt Claire and Maya by their arms and were walking them quickly down the hall with flashlights.

When the lights came on, they looked up and down the hallway. She turned the lights off and on three times, hoping Aunt Claire and Maya might guess it was her, then she gave the computer a new command. The fire sprinklers suddenly burst to life, spraying water everywhere. The guards let go, and Maya and Aunt Claire ran. They did know it was her.

Isabel turned on the lights in the hallway to the left, hoping they'd follow. They did. She continued to light their way, leading them to Sara and Andrew. Once the four of them were inside, she locked them in.

She sighed, relieved they were together and safe. All of them but her.

"Now what?" she asked herself.

SHE NEEDN'T HAVE ASKED. Seconds later, Bruce and a group of men appeared on the screen and pounded on the door. Everyone was looking around for another way out. They backed into a corner. Andrew broke the glass on the fire extinguisher in the room and held it in front of them like a weapon.

"You can't get in," she told them. She shut the lights off in the hallway. Flashlights clicked on. It was hard to tell what was happening, but the lights appeared to move back. Then something flashed. Again. And again.

A gun.

The door swung open. Bruce held his gun out in front of him and stormed in.

Andrew set down the fire extinguisher and put his hands up. He stood in front of the others. Bruce grabbed him by the arm. The other guards moved around them all and took them by the arms. Maya resisted, but only for a moment because Bruce displayed his gun again.

Suddenly the intercom dinged pleasantly above Isabel's head. "Ding, ding, ding, ding."

"Hello, Isabel," said Dr. Rodriguez. "You sure are a clever girl. Perhaps too clever for your own good."

Isabel sat perfectly still. Her stomach rumbled with nerves.

"I am tired of messing around now. This could have been easy. This could have been *so* easy, but you have all made it this way. I will get this information from you by whatever means necessary. Isabel, I have your aunt, your sister, and your friends. They aren't going anywhere, and we are going to find you. If you would like to come to us, that will make things better for you, but if you want to keep hiding, keep messing around, it is only a matter of time before we find you and bring you here. And I will make you pay for that."

The voice stopped.

Isabel bit her lower lip. She watched as they shoved her family and friends back into the room with Herbert. Guards stood all around them. Another group set off down the hallway, sweeping rooms along the way, looking for her.

She took a deep breath. She turned all the lights back on throughout the buildings. Her hands shook as she reached for the doorknob and opened the office door.

She took slow and deliberate steps for the door, expecting someone to jump out and grab her at any moment, but no one did. They must all be in the main building. She headed for the exit.

She felt sick to her stomach. *I hope this is the right decision*, she thought as she pushed the door open. She stepped outside. It was still dark, though it was nearing sunrise. As she walked between the bushes, she startled when she heard someone whisper.

"Isabel! Isabel! Over here!" She looked toward the bushes on the side of the building. Officer Williams was crouched behind a shrub.

"Officer Williams. We need help."

"I know, I know. I heard everything," he said.

"How did you get in here?"

"The guards are panicking over there. I sent some of my officers to try to get in, and while they distracted the guards, I sneaked in on foot."

Isabel nodded.

"Go," he said. "Turn yourself in. They don't know I'm here, so I'll help you guys as soon as I can get more resources. For now, just do what they ask."

"I'm so glad you believe us now."

"I'm sorry I didn't before. Although I'm still not so sure about this talking dog thing."

Isabel smiled tightly.

"Be careful," Officer Williams said.

ABOUT 200 FEET from the door to the main building, the guards spotted Isabel. They ran toward her, tasers out. She put her hands in the air like a criminal. One of them grabbed her firmly by the upper arm, digging his fingers into her skin. She winced, but he held tighter. She told herself to be strong.

They marched her through the hallways, and she held her head high.

"You really made a mess here," one of the guards said as they stepped onto the linoleum. "Bruce is not happy. You'd better do what they say."

She looked up at the man. He looked down at her with big round eyes, almost remorseful.

"I'm just a kid," she said. "A kid with dead parents. And you guys kidnapped the only family I have."

"That's enough," said the man on the other side of her.

They walked in silence the rest of the way, but the nicer man loosened his grip.

Inside the room, Aunt Claire ran for her. The guards let her. She wrapped her arms tightly around Isabel and squeezed. Isabel hid her face in Aunt Claire's neck and, even if it was just for a second, she savored the comfort before the guards pulled them apart.

Isabel looked over at Maya. Her face looked drawn, and her shoulders sagged. Her normally strong and muscular sister looked meek and worn down. Sara reached out and squeezed Isabel's hand reassuringly.

At least we are all together, thought Isabel.

Dr. Rodriguez walked in.

"Steve," started Aunt Claire. "Steve, be reasonable. These are kids. They don't know anything about genetic modification. They can't help you at all. Let these kids go. I will help you. I'll give you what you want."

"Yes, you will," Steve snapped. "You will give me what I want. You've made this entirely too difficult, Claire. And the kids have stood in my way and disrupted my plans every step of the way. You think I'm just going to let them walk out of here? Walk out and go to the police? Walk out and hack into my lab again?"

Everyone stood by silently.

"There is only one way that any of you are walking out of here!" he shouted.

Aunt Claire's cheeks were flushed, and her eyes were

watery. She took a deep breath and closed her eyes for a moment. "Let me see your work so far."

"Don't do it, Aunt Claire!" Isabel screamed. Maya grabbed her. "Let me go. Stop, Aunt Claire! Don't do it!"

Maya pulled her back hard.

"Stop it, Maya."

"Isabel. Please. We have no choice."

Aunt Claire stepped forward toward Dr. Rodriguez. He pulled out a chair for her in front of a large desk. He pulled open a notebook with a diagram of DNA printed on it. Aunt Claire squinted and looked down at it. She traced her fingers along one side of the DNA strand, mumbling something to herself that Isabel couldn't understand.

Dr. Rodriguez leaned over her, practically drooling as Aunt Claire reviewed his data.

"What are you trying to do here?" She pointed to a spot on the diagram. "What kind of modification are you making here?"

"Strength. Aggression. Endurance," Dr. Rodriguez stated, a sly smile curling on the sides of his mouth.

Aunt Claire looked up at him with pleading eyes. "What for?"

Dr. Rodriguez smiled. "War."

"War? What do you mean *war*?"

"It's a revolution," he said. "We've had service animals as soldiers for years. We could have super soldiers. Animals that have better senses and more power than men do."

"Animals that are *weapons*?"

Dr. Rodriguez nodded. "Weapons that can be sold to the highest bidder."

"The highest bidder? You mean, not the government? Not *our* government?"

"I mean the highest bidder."

"You would sell these animals to bad guys?" Sara asked. "To tyrants or dictators? Or terrorists?!"

"If I don't, someone else will. It's just a matter of who has the technology available first."

"This isn't technology," said Aunt Claire. "These are animals. Living, breathing, thinking animals."

"They're dogs, Claire."

Aunt Claire stared up at him, shocked.

Isabel tried to comprehend the idea of dogs being turned into weapons that were handed over to terrorists. She thought of the soldiers who train their dogs for years to work together. She thought of the brave men and women fighting to keep their country safe. She thought of the bombings she'd seen on the news. What had seemed so far away before seemed to be resting on her shoulders now. Aunt Claire could not help them. Isabel wouldn't let her.

"Stop, Aunt Claire," she said. "Do not help him."

Everyone turned to face Isabel.

"Stop," said Herbert. Isabel turned and gave him a sad smile.

"There's nothing he can do to us that's so bad that it makes helping him worth it," Isabel continued.

Dr. Rodriguez spun around and faced her.

"I've had enough of you. Bruce."

Isabel swallowed hard. Bruce stepped forward.

Maya stepped in front of Isabel. She squared her shoulders and held her head high, challenging Bruce. He sneered at her and stepped forward. As soon as he got close enough, he swung at Maya. With just one punch, he knocked her over. She landed hard on some equipment.

Isabel stepped backwards, just out of Bruce's reach. He reached toward her, but she moved sideways so he grabbed at nothing, throwing him off balance.

She slipped right past him and ran toward Aunt Claire. She dove at the computer tower on the desk and hit it hard, knocking it to the floor and sending pieces scattering all around them.

Dr. Rodriguez suddenly started laughing.

"Come on, aren't you the programmer? You know we don't house the data on this computer alone. It's stored on our network."

Of course, she knew that, but she'd hoped to buy them some time—more specifically, to buy Officer Williams some time.

She stared at Dr. Rodriguez, waiting for him to say more, when Bruce's arms snaked hard around her. He lifted her up in the air as she screamed and kicked.

Two more security guards rushed in and helped Bruce restrain Isabel, zip-tying her hands and feet again before throwing her to the ground.

"You're really getting on my nerves, kid," Bruce whispered sternly in her ear. "Give me a reason, and I'll make you wish you never showed up here."

Isabel's head ached, and she could taste blood. Lying on her side on the ground, she looked up to see Aunt Claire and Maya being held back by security as they fought to get to her. She rolled onto her back and stared up at the ceiling. She was dizzy, and the throb in her head felt like thunder. Then, everything went dark.

SIXTEEN

Isabel was walking through the hallways of her old house. A volleyball rolled into the hallway from her sister's room. Isabel poked her head in. Maya was talking on the phone.

She continued down the hallway to the kitchen. Music met her ears. She peeked around the corner and saw Mom and Dad. They were in the kitchen together, doing the dishes the way they used to. Dad took some soapy bubbles from the sink and wiped them on Mom's nose. She giggled at him and playfully whacked him with the dishcloth before wiping the bubbles off. Isabel watched them patiently. She felt like she could stand there forever.

Dad noticed her first. He smiled widely at her and reached out with one arm to draw Isabel to him. Mom turned and smiled, and the three of them all hugged each other. Isabel closed her eyes and leaned into her mom, smelling her sweet shampoo, and feeling the softness of her skin. She felt the strength of her parents' love as they held onto her. She was safe. She was happy. She savored it.

The music stopped slowly, and Isabel opened her eyes.

"Izzie," Dad said. "Don't give up. Don't ever give up."

"I don't know what else to do."

"You'll think of something," said Mom. "You always do. You're the cleverest girl I have ever known."

Isabel looked into her eyes. She looked just like Maya.

"But how do we get away," she begged.

"Maybe you don't," Mom said.

"Time to wake up," Dad said.

"I don't want to. I want to stay here with you."

"Wake up," said Mom. "Claire and Maya need you."

"I need *you*. I need both of you."

"Wake up, Izzie," said Dad.

"Wake up."

"Wake up."

"Come on, wake up."

Isabel groaned and turned her head from side to side.

"Mom."

"Isabel, wake up. Wake up."

She opened her eyes. Maya was kneeling over her. Her face was drawn into a deep frown. Aunt Claire was kneeling on her other side.

Isabel blinked a few times. Maya sighed with relief.

"Come on." Aunt Claire helped her sit up. "There you go. Are you okay? How's your head?"

Isabel didn't answer. She looked around. Bruce was standing nearby with his arms crossed. Sara and Andrew were huddled together where they stood before.

Aunt Claire turned on Dr. Rodriguez. "You're a monster. These are kids."

Dr. Rodriguez pursed his lips. His eyebrows were drawn together and down. He motioned for Bruce to get Isabel.

"You will do what I asked, Claire."

"You will never get away with this," shouted Isabel,

sitting and fighting with the zip ties. "The police know all about it. They're going to stop you."

Dr. Rodriguez laughed. "The police? You mean Officer Williams, who we caught in the bushes a few minutes ago? I'm not all that worried about him."

Isabel was sick to her stomach. Her shoulders fell, and her body felt weak.

"What have you done with him?" she asked.

"You'll never get away with this, Steve," Aunt Claire pleaded. "Kidnapping kids? Kidnapping cops? How do you think this will end?"

"I know exactly how it will end." He smirked at her. "My helicopter is fueled up and ready. When I have what I need, I will leave, and none of these podunk cops will ever find me."

The guards glanced at each other nervously. Isabel assumed they weren't in on this escape plan and wondered what that meant for them.

"Claire, I believe we were in the middle of something here," said Dr. Rodriguez as he pulled out the chair.

Aunt Claire stood up slowly. She looked at Maya, then at Isabel. Tears welled in her eyes. Isabel thought it must be torture to have to choose between your life's work and your family. She didn't blame her for giving in.

Aunt Claire walked over to the desk and sat down.

As Aunt Claire asked Dr. Rodriguez questions she couldn't understand, Isabel turned her attention back to the others. Aunt Claire was clearly delaying. She asked the same question different ways. Dr. Rodriguez was growing annoyed.

Isabel scooted on her butt until she was up against the wall. She leaned against it, letting her shoulders relax.

"Are you guys okay?" she asked Andrew and Sara. They both nodded. "I'm sorry we got you into this."

"Let's just focus on getting us all out of this," Andrew said.

"Maybe we don't get out of this," said Isabel suddenly, remembering what Mom had said in her dream. Her eyes went wide, and she looked up. "Maybe we stay right here."

They looked at her like she might be crazy. The huddled around her, and she spoke quietly.

"We've got to ruin this. If we can't fight our way out, we have to destroy it from in here."

"How do we do that?" Maya whispered.

Isabel looked at Aunt Claire, who was studying some data quietly.

"You have to do it, Maya. I'm going to get Bruce to hit me again, then you need to say that you'll tell them everything. But you've got to mess it up—tell them the wrong things, lead them off course."

"That's perfect," Andrew said. "But I'll do it. You've been hit enough."

Isabel considered protesting but she really didn't know if she could take another blow and still be useful.

"But I don't know anything about this stuff," Maya protested.

"Fake it," said Andrew. "Tell them you don't understand it, but you'll tell them what you've seen in her lab."

Maya nodded.

"You've got to act really upset when he hits Andrew, so they're convinced you gave in," Sara said.

"I don't have to act for that."

Andrew stood up. He squared his shoulders and took a step forward.

"You need to let these girls go," he demanded. Dr. Rodriguez didn't even look up. Bruce stepped forward. "They need medical attention. I demand that you let them go."

"Why should I do that?"

"You've already beat on them enough. You're getting what you want from Claire. Let them go. Now."

Bruce smiled and stepped forward.

"Or what?"

Andrew stepped forward fast. His athletic stature on full display as he puffed out his chest. He shoved Bruce. He didn't even budge.

In one quick, fluid movement, Bruce drew back and punched Andrew. He fell like a box of rocks. Right on cue, Maya jumped up.

"Stop! Stop! Please don't hurt him!"

This got the doctor's attention.

"Please stop this. Don't hurt them. I'll tell you everything. I can tell you what I saw. I watched her do experiments."

Dr. Rodriguez stood up and strode toward her.

"Finally. One of you has come to her senses."

"Yes, I'll tell you. It's not worth hurting them."

"I guess all we had to do was hit your boyfriend, and you'd come around. I wish I would have known that sooner. We could have saved a lot of time."

Isabel watched intently. Maya was doing a great job. Andrew was laying on the ground with his nose bleeding. She caught his eye, and he winked at her. She leaned over toward Sara and nudged her. Sara nodded slightly. The plan was working.

"I saw a drawing like this," said Maya, pointing at a diagram. "But part of it was purple."

"What part?" Dr. Rodriguez was practically jumping up and down.

Maya picked up the diagram, turning it this way and that.

"Just this one side," she said, tracing her arm along some line.

Aunt Claire pulled a face. She narrowed her eyes and cocked her head to one side. She almost interrupted but stopped herself and looked at Isabel.

As subtly as possible Isabel winked at Aunt Claire.

Unfortunately, Bruce saw her.

"What's going on here," he said. "Dr. Rodriguez..."

"Not now!" he shouted back.

Isabel turned her gaze toward Maya. Aunt Claire looked at the ground.

Bruce looked at each of them, then back at Maya.

"Yes, yes. This is it," Maya said. "It looked just like this."

Dr. Rodriguez was eagerly writing something down.

"What about the computer," he asked her. "Can you get the information out of the system?"

Maya looked at Isabel.

"No, I can't. I don't know anything about programming."

"Never mind, never mind." He said, pulling documents out of a file and shoving them in front of her.

Aunt Claire kept stepping closer and closer to Maya. She seemed to be catching on.

Isabel squirmed in her zip ties. Her sides ached from the awkward way she was sitting. If Maya pulled this off and they gave Dr. Rodriguez the wrong information, he could never do what he planned.

"She's lying," Bruce said calmly. "She doesn't know what she's talking about."

Dr. Rodriguez looked at Maya, then back at Bruce.

Suddenly Andrew came out of nowhere and hit Bruce. He tackled him. Bruce hit the ground hard, and Andrew jumped up. Bruce was much bigger, but Andrew was obviously faster. He grabbed Isabel and threw her over his shoulder. Herbert barked like crazy. Maya, realizing what was happening, shoved Dr. Rodriguez hard. He stumbled into a wall and fell to the ground. Maya yelled for Sara, who was opening Herbert's kennel.

Aunt Claire rushed to the door and held it open. The five of them and Herbert ran from the room and turned down a hallway. *So much for staying put*, thought Isabel, hoping this time they'd have better luck.

Isabel tried to hold onto Andrew as he ran, but with her hands and feet bound, she mostly just bounced around. She looked up and realized where they were.

"Turn here!"

Everyone flew around the corner.

"Go through the open double doors," she yelled. As soon as Andrew was through, Maya closed the doors behind them. They were back in the room with the kennels, though they were all empty now. Sara and Maya barricaded the door. Aunt Claire was searching through cabinet drawers. She returned with a letter opener and began sawing away at the zip ties that bound Isabel.

"Isabel, there's no way out of this room." Aunt Claire looked terrified. "Why did you bring us in here?"

As soon as her feet were free, Isabel stood up and walked over to the cabinet where she hid earlier. She pulled her backpack out and placed her laptop on the counter.

"We only have to stay in here long enough for help to come," she said. She logged into the network and opened Skype to call 911. She got through to the dispatcher.

"Are you guys okay?" the woman asked when Isabel identified herself.

"We are locked in a room in Gennovations. I think they have Officer Williams in custody."

"We already have all units en route."

"I think you should call in some reinforcements. Can you contact the county or something?"

"Already did. Help is coming. Just stay put."

Andrew threw one arm around Sara and one around Maya. Big smiles grew across their faces. Aunt Claire sighed and slumped against the counter, and Herbert nuzzled her.

"Are you and Officer Gonzalez okay?" Maya asked, remembering that the dispatcher and Officer had been hurt in the kidnapping.

"I'm okay, just a little beat up. Officer Gonzalez is already out there."

Isabel was flooded with relief. They were going to be fine, and they hadn't given anything up to Dr. Rodriguez. The good guys win.

Happy to wait it out, the group all sat down around the room. Isabel told them how she found this room earlier and what she had found in it. Aunt Claire looked at her curiously.

"Those poor animals," she said.

Everyone nodded.

"Not only were they experimented on, but they were neglected. I gave them just a tiny bit of attention, and they reacted."

Aunt Claire nodded.

"Once the police get here, I'll try to help get them all rounded up."

"No," said Herbert.

"Oh, don't be jealous." Aunt Claire scratched rubbed his belly. "How was Daisy?"

"She was fine. I'm sure she's eaten our couch by now."

Everyone laughed, until they noticed the smoke.

"No," said Herbert again.

SEVENTEEN

It started in the back corner of the room. Smoke began to billow in from under the wall.

"They're trying to force us out of the room!" yelled Maya.

Flames began to creep up the bottom of the wall. The guards had set the exterior wall on fire, forcing the group away from it and toward the exit.

Andrew ran around frantically looking for an extinguisher or something to hold water. Maya found a bucket in a cabinet, and they filled it at the sink. By the time it was full, it was too late, flames grew across the wall. Aunt Claire pushed Isabel and Sara toward the door.

"We can't go out there. They're going to be waiting right outside," said Isabel.

"We have no choice," Aunt Claire responded. Isabel and Sara moved up against the door, waiting in case the others could get the fire under control. Herbert huddled behind them. Isabel watched in horror as the others tried to do something. Aunt Claire, Maya, and Andrew ran around, panicked, and yelled to each other, but they could not slow the fire. Isabel rushed forward and grabbed her backpack again. She shoved her laptop in before returning to Sara. Sara stared at her with tears in her eyes.

"What do we do, Izzie?"

"We have to go," she said. "We should try running in different directions, but I'm sure there are a bunch of people waiting for us on the other side of this door."

Sara nodded. She reached down and squeezed Isabel's hand.

Aunt Claire turned around. She looked at Sara and Isabel, then back to the fire, then at Maya and Andrew. Flames were spreading rapidly. Half of the room was engulfed, and the smoke was growing thick.

"It's no use. We have to go."

Maya started coughing.

"Maya, come on!" Aunt Claire shouted. She turned to Sara and Isabel and pushed them toward the door. "Go now!"

Sara grabbed Isabel by the arm and yanked her through the door. Smoke rushed into the hall, blocking Isabel's vision. Someone grabbed Isabel and she heard Sara scream.

Isabel kicked and scratched but it was no use. She could hardly breath, and the men were so strong.

Guards were rushing into the room. One grabbed Aunt Claire and two went for Andrew. Herbert dashed away between the legs of the guards.

Maya saw the guards coming her way and took a fighter's stance. She wasn't going down without a fight. But as she moved forward, a loud crack sounded from the ceiling. Isabel looked up just in time to see a beam fall.

Maya was trapped behind the beam. She dove to the side to move around it, but part of the ceiling fell toward her. The guards stepped backwards, away from Maya and the fire. Another loud crack sounded, and another beam fell, blocking Isabel's view of her sister. Isabel screamed for Maya, but she couldn't see her.

Guards pulled Isabel away. She fought them, turning back to try to see her sister. Flames rose all around them, and they dragged Isabel down the hall.

―――――

THEY TOOK ISABEL AWAY ALONE. She fought them, but it was no use. Two men had her by the arms. They walked her into another building, to a small office with no windows and shoved her inside. She fell hard into a desk.

"Stay put," one of them said. "We are almost out of time, and we are tired of you messing this up."

The other man walked over to the desk and ripped the computer tower from the ground, breaking cords. He carried it outside of the office.

"We will be right outside this door. Both of us."

He slammed the door behind him, leaving Isabel alone in the dark. It was cold in the office. Isabel wrapped her arms around herself. Her body and her head ached from being beat up earlier. She touched a bruise on her lip and flinched away from the pain. A slow tear ran down her cheek. She pulled her knees to her chest and tried to think, but the tears started coming more quickly. Her shoulders shook and her nose ran as she sobbed, gasping for breath.

Maya didn't make it, she thought. She turned to the side and threw up on the floor. After retching a few minutes, she sat with her back against the wall and wiped her face with her shirt.

She was out of ideas. She didn't know if any of her ideas ever mattered. If they'd just stayed home and let the police handle it, Maya would be alive. If Aunt Claire hadn't trusted Isabel to know her secret, Maya would be alive. If her mom and dad had not driven that day, they would be alive. If she, Isabel, hadn't screwed everything up, her whole family would be alive.

She thought back to all the times they'd fought. She had wasted so much time arguing with Maya and so much time being angry over nothing. She'd been a terrible sister. A terrible person.

"It's all my fault," she whispered into the lonely room.

She wondered what had happened to Aunt Claire. What had happened to Andrew and Sara? What had happened to Officer Williams? The animals?

Realizing she had her backpack and laptop, she perked up a moment, but then doubted she could do much with it. She slipped it out of her backpack. It was banged up but powered on.

She had network access, which surprised her. Greg must have cleared the way for her. She pulled up the security feeds. She scrolled from room to room and didn't see a soul. She moved to the hallway outside the kennel room. The fire was out, but the room was destroyed. She couldn't make out anything in the room at all. Something moved, and she squinted, but it was simply the wind moving the debris around. She struggled to pull her eyes away.

She took a deep breath and closed her eyes as she pushed the arrow key, moving to the next camera. This time she saw motion, but it wasn't a person. The glow-in-dark snake slithered down the hallway.

"You haven't escaped yet, either?" She sure hoped he made it out and fared better than she had.

The snake slithered to the end of the hall, where a closed door blocked his path. He explored around a bit before realizing he had hit a dead end and turning back the other way.

A notification popped up on screen asking her to allow Skype to update.

She pulled her eyebrows together. She still had Skype. She opened the program and tried to call 911 again. To her surprise it started to ring. The dispatcher from earlier answered, sounding frightened.

"It's me. Isabel. We need help." she whispered directly into the microphone.

"Isabel. Where are you? Are you still at Gennovations?"

"Yes. I'm in an office. There was a fire. My sister was in the fire."

The computer was silent.

"Hello? Did you hear me? Maya was in the fire."

"I'm sending an ambulance, Isabel, but they can't get in. Gennovations has blocked all the gates. They are insisting that you aren't in there and are refusing to open the gates or turn off the electric fence. We can't see anything, and we can't talk to Officer Williams, so we are trying to get a search warrant signed. If they won't let us through, we will start arresting the guards, but you have to hang in there a little longer. Find a place to hide."

Before Isabel could respond, the door swung open, and one of the guards stormed in.

He grabbed Isabel's computer from her and slammed it shut. Then he turned and smashed it into a filing cabinet over and over again until it was a mess of pieces on the ground. Without a word, he stormed out of the office and slammed the door again.

Isabel curled up in a little ball on the ground, deciding to just wait for whatever would happen next.

Then she heard voices.

EIGHTEEN

Isabel scooted close to the door and pushed her ear against it.

"Yes, I understand this is what you were told. I'm telling you something else," a man said.

"We have to keep her here."

"I need her in the control room. You can come with her, whatever, but we need her in there to get into the program Dr. Rodriguez is accessing. Don't make me go and get Bruce."

A few seconds later, the door creaked open.

"Isabel?" a head peeked around the corner, and she met Greg's eyes. He looked different. His hair was messed up, and his clothes were disheveled. He winked at her. "You will come to the control room now. Let's go."

Isabel stood up quickly. She nodded at him. She understood.

"I'm not helping you," she yelled. "How many times do I have to tell you people? I'll never help you!"

"You will." He grabbed her by the arm and pulled her hard toward him. "Let's go."

She and Greg started down the hallway, the security guards close on their heels. Greg squeezed her arm twice, a signal that he had a plan. She continued to pretend to resist him as they walked, pulling herself away and shooting him dirty looks while he yanked her around by her arm. They arrived at the control room, the same room where she had met Greg, and he pushed the door open.

"Sit here." He shoved her toward a workstation. "And power that computer up."

She sat still and stared at him defiantly.

"Power it up!" he screamed.

Isabel sighed dramatically before turning the computer on and turning toward the screen.

"We need to look at the back end of an HTML code," he said. He walked toward her and leaned over her to use the mouse. He opened a .txt document, which had line after line of simple code. It was just a document, which did nothing, but she doubted the guards would know that. After looking at it a moment, Isabel realized it was nothing more than a simple list.

The security guards stepped close and occasionally peered over her shoulder, but it was obvious that neither of them knew what they were looking at.

"See here," Greg said, pointing to a line of code, midway down the page. Isabel stared at it for just a second before realizing what he had done. In each line Isabel spotted an error, after the error he had typed a word. The line where he pointed said, "Where." She followed his logic downwards and found the sentence

Where

R

the

Others

"Your prompt is wrong here," she said taking control of the mouse and moving the cursor. She typed "?"

"What about here?" He pointed to another section of code, where he had done the same thing. It read

R

U

HURT

She gently shook her head, took back the mouse and keyboard and on three separate lines typed

MA

YA

?

Greg suddenly stood up and looked at the guards.

"Do either of you know where Dr. Rodriguez is working? I need to refresh his program to see if these changes worked."

The men looked at each other.

"I'll go," said one. "Keep a close eye on the girl."

The man walked out of the room.

Isabel turned back to the screen. Greg had also typed, throughout various lines

DIS

TRACT

HIM

Isabel suddenly jumped up. "Where is my sister? Where is my aunt? What have you done?"

The guard moved close to Isabel, ready to grab her. While he was watching Isabel, Greg pulled out a can of pepper spray and shot him in the face. The man screamed and grabbed his face. Isabel rushed toward him and knocked him down.

"We have to tie him up!" Greg shouted. He reached in a drawer and pulled out the horse leads Isabel had used earlier. The two worked quickly, sitting on the man as they fought to tie his arms and legs. They succeeded and stepped back though the man fought, trying to free himself.

"Help me roll him into the server room."

Isabel squatted down and pushed with all her might. She and Greg pushed until the man was almost all the way inside, then Greg pushed the door shut.

Breathless, Isabel looked up at Greg.

"Thank you."

"Don't thank me. I am so sorry I was involved with this. I had no idea what was going on. They just told me that this was important medical data, and some practical joker kid had hacked it. This is way, way more than I bargained for."

"Do you know where my family is? What happened to my sister?"

"I don't know. I'm sorry. But I do know where they took the others. If we hurry, we can find them."

"No. I'll hurry. You stay here and help me."

Greg smiled. "You got it."

He rushed over to the computer and typed in some information.

"Okay, Isabel. All the doors but that one are locked. I will light your way—that's a trick I learned from you."

Isabel smiled, then without warning, she wrapped her arms around Greg. It felt remarkable to have someone hug her in that moment.

"Thank you," she said into his chest.

"Go."

ISABEL RAN DOWN THE HALL. The lights were on to her left, so she went that way. She found she was going right and left so many times she was disoriented again.

She reached the end of the hallway, but no lights came on for her to follow. She looked around, then the lights blinked off and on three times.

They must be in this hallway, she thought.

She began looking through windows. Finally, the third door down, she saw Sara inside and pulled the door open.

Andrew and Sara looked up suddenly when she walked in. Their faces, a mixture of fear and anger, quickly changed to relief. They rushed toward her and wrapped her into an enormous hug.

"Maya? Do you guys know what happened to Maya?"

Sara bit her lip. Andrew shook his head slowly.

"I'm sorry, but they pulled us away so fast." He looked at the ground. "I truly don't know."

Isabel couldn't speak. She nodded her head twice.

"But Maya is probably fine. I mean, she's fast and strong." Andrew didn't sound like he had even convinced himself.

"What should we do, Isabel?"

"We have to get out of here," Isabel replied to Sara. "Luckily, I have some help now."

She walked to the door again and pulled it open. She peeked her head out the door and looked both ways.

"Come on," she said. "Let's hurry. We can try to get to the guard gate. The police are there."

Andrew and Sara followed her, amazed the lights turned on in front of them then turned off behind them. They jogged down the hallways, zigging and zagging.

They ran around the corner into an area that must serve as a lobby. The space was wide open with a desk in the middle. Hallways on both sides of the room led off in separate directions. One whole wall was floor-to-ceiling glass panels with glass double doors in the center.

They stopped and looked around, nervous to step out into the open. Andrew stepped forward first, walking toward the double doors. As soon as he did, footsteps sounded, and Bruce appeared out of the shadows with a menacing smile on his face.

NINETEEN

Isabel grabbed Sara and pulled her back into the hallway, where they might still be hidden.

"How did you get out here? And where's the other girl?"

"I... I... I don't know. The door opened so I ran."

"No, you didn't. You're the big brother. You didn't leave your sister behind."

Bruce stepped forward toward where the girls were standing.

"I did. I was going for help. I don't know where she is. I think still in the room where you locked us in."

Bruce looked at him skeptically. "Sure."

He continued toward the girls, the silence broken up only by his footsteps. Isabel and Sara clung to each other and held their breath. Isabel saw that Sara had her eyes closed tightly. The moments seemed to drag on forever until they heard a low, deep growl.

Isabel's head snapped up, just as Bruce's did. The big, muscular dog that Isabel befriended had stepped out from one of the other hallways. It stalked toward Bruce, teeth bared and ears pinned.

The dog stepped in between the girls and Bruce. Slowly, Bruce reached for his waist to pull out a weapon, but before he could, the dog lunged at him. Bruce put his hands up to protect himself, but the dog tackled him.

Sara pulled on Isabel's wrist, dragging her toward the doors and Andrew.

The doors were locked but Andrew threw a heavy chair into one of them and the glass shattered. The three squeezed through and outside.

The sun was up, shining brightly, but the cold stung Isabel as she looked around, trying to find the guard gate.

"Where are we?" she yelled.

"Come on. We'll follow this driveway." Andrew began running through a parking lot to a paved road. The girls followed closely behind him, holding onto each other.

They could hear the sounds of people talking, yelling nearby.

"We must be close," Sara said.

Then they all heard a scream.

"That was Aunt Claire," said Isabel. "We have to go back."

"No, let's go to the police. They can help," said Andrew.

"There might not be time." Isabel turned and ran the other way. "You go. Find the police. I'll find Aunt Claire."

Andrew and Sara both followed.

"You're not going back alone," Sara panted behind her.

"We are with you," Andrew added. "All the way."

As they approached the sound of the voices, they slowed down. They tucked themselves behind a building and looked around the corner. Dr. Rodriguez was dragging Aunt Claire through the open space toward the warehouse building. She kicked and screamed but he had her by the hair.

"Let's hope I still have help," Isabel said, spotting the camera above them. She waved at the camera for a few seconds. The outdoor light next to them blinked on and off three times. She pointed toward the warehouse and ran toward it as quietly as she could, hoping she still had surprise on her side.

When they reached the warehouse, the door was open. They slipped inside. Aunt Claire was still screaming so they were able to move quickly without being heard.

They hid behind a pallet and watched.

"I'm not going with you!"

"You are. We can't stay here. The place almost burned down, and the police are practically banging the doors down."

"Give it up, Steve! It's over!"

"It's not over. You're coming with me, and you're going to help me with this research."

"I won't."

"You will, Claire. If you don't, you'll have no family to go back to. I underestimated your family once, but I won't do it again."

"Too bad you *did* do it again," said Isabel, stepping out from behind the pallet.

Dr. Rodriguez looked up at her. His eyes were wide, and his mouth dropped open.

"She's right. The police are here. All your cronies are gone. It's over."

"Wow." Dr, Rodriquez smiled. "You just never learn, do you?"

Isabel puffed out her chest. She was determined to hold her ground.

"You can't hurt me," she spat at him. "If you do, you'll never get what you want."

He seemed to consider this.

"You're right." He laughed gently. "I've been going about this all wrong."

He lunged forward and grabbed Isabel by the hair. Isabel's yell was overpowered by a loud engine sound. She could see through the windows that a helicopter was waiting in the clearing, its blade sending dust and leaves up into the air.

"Okay, Claire. I'm taking your niece with me. I'll take her wherever I please."

Aunt Claire's face was pure terror.

"Please!" she yelled over the noise. "Please, Steve! Stop this!"

He pulled Isabel toward a rolling door, and he pushed a button to open it. It started to open but stopped. He tried again. It didn't work. He moved over to the next rolling door and the same thing happened.

Greg, thought Isabel. This was her chance. She had to make her move now.

She slammed her body into Dr. Rodriguez as hard as she could, throwing him off balance. A rolling door a few doors down opened and then began to close.

"This way!" she screamed. She ran toward the door and slid under it. Sara slid under then Andrew. Aunt Claire was almost through when she screamed again.

Dr. Rodriguez had one of her arms and was pulling her back into the building. Isabel, Andrew and Sara pulled on her the other way. At the last second, Aunt Claire got her arm lose and pulled it under the door.

"Run!" she yelled. As a side door swung open on the other end of the wall and Dr. Rodriquez ran out, Sara tripped and fell. Andrew stopped and went back for her. He pulled her to her feet, and they continued through the woods. Suddenly, another door opened on a nearby building and a bunch of security guards ran out. They came at them from the side. Isabel ducked in between some trees, and the others followed as they tried to fight their way through the brush.

She thought the gate was directly in front of her. She tried to move toward them, forcing herself to keep going even though she realized she'd lost sight of all the others.

Isabel ducked behind a tree and held her breath, listening for footsteps or screams. She could not have gotten this far away from all of them yet. She must have gone the wrong way.

She heard a twig snap. Someone was coming. Isabel held her breath and bit her lip. Sweat covered her face and dripped down her forehead despite the cold weather. Her heartbeat pounded loudly in her ears.

"Isabelllllll," sang Dr. Rodriguez. "I know you're here, Isabel."

Another few footsteps indicated he was getting closer.

"You and I are going to get out of this place," he said. "We are going to work through some of these... let's call them *challenges*."

He stepped even closer.

"I need your help and I know, after what happened to your sister, that your aunt will do absolutely anything to keep you safe. Let's just make sure she does that, okay?"

He was only a few feet away now, looking around trees to his right and left. It was only a matter of seconds before he found her. She clenched her fists, held her breath, and waited.

"Stop right there!" someone shouted.

Dr. Rodriguez looked behind him. Officer Williams was standing behind him, his hand resting on his belt.

Dr. Rodriquez laughed. "Or else? I know you don't have your weapon. I took it from you myself, Officer."

Officer Williams stepped forward, his shoulders back, his chest out. "You are under arrest—"

He laughed again, interrupting the officer. "You can't take me anywhere. You have no gun, no handcuffs. You don't even have a badge, and after my lawyer gets done with you, you may never have a badge again."

"You won't get away with this."

"Of course, I will. Even if you could arrest me, I have the best attorneys in the world. They would have me free and clear in no time. Don't even waste your time."

Isabel knew better than to wait around while these two argued. She tiptoed out from behind the tree and moved along the woods behind where Dr. Rodriguez was, hoping he wouldn't turn around. As soon as she got far enough away that she thought it was safe to do so, she took off running. She heard the men yelling, then a series of bangs and thuds. They must be fighting. When she emerged from the woods, she was completely lost. She had no idea which way would lead her to the guard gates and which would lead her back to the security guards.

She tried to calm down, taking deep breaths and focusing her thoughts. She had a stitch in her side from sprinting. If only she'd had Maya's athleticism.

She had no choice but to roll the dice. She turned left and walked through the trees. As she emerged, she realized she'd gone away from the gates. But she saw something much worse.

Sara, Andrew, and Aunt Claire were all on their knees, with their hands behind them. Their breath was visible in the cold air. They were all still catching their breath from running around. Several security guards stood over them and paced behind and in front of them.

"No," said someone quietly. She turned around and saw Herbert standing in the woods nearby. When she looked up at him, he wagged his tail. Behind him, stepped another dog from the lab. Then another. Then another. Isabel noticed that the big dog who had saved her from Bruce was missing. As she approached them quietly, she saw quick movement from behind Herbert. She jumped back, but then Freddie bounded toward her.

"Freddie?" She scratched him behind the ears. "How did you get here?"

A moment later, Nolan landed on a branch near Isabel.

"How on earth did you two get here? How did you find us?"

"Stop," said Herbert.

"Okay guys, I need your help. I have no idea if you can understand me, but we have to try."

She looked around at the dogs. They all seemed to be listening. She tried to think of the most logical plan, and it was as simple as it was effective: a stampede. She was willing to bet that all these animals would protect Aunt Claire.

"Okay, everyone, follow me. We are going to run over there and cause some chaos so everyone can get away."

She stepped forward one step. All the dogs followed.

"Here we go," she said and started jogging toward her friends. The dogs followed closely, and when they approached Aunt Claire and the others, they bounded past her. The dogs ran in circles around the security guards, jumping on them, and biting their pant legs. They growled and backed them away from Aunt Claire. Nolan flew low, diving at their heads.

"Come on!" Isabel screamed. The others looked up at her. They jumped to their feet and ran as quickly as they could. Fortunately, their hands weren't bound.

The group ran through the open space, along the path toward the gates. Isabel could see the gate ahead of her. In what seemed like slow motion, the gates swung open, and police cruisers rushed in. Red and blue flashing lights surrounded them.

Andrew quickly rushed to his sister and wrapped his arms around her.

Someone called for an ambulance. Isabel felt gentle arms pull her back as the officers and medics looked at Aunt Claire. Isabel turned and realized the arms were Lisa's. She wrapped Isabel into a gentle hug. Isabel started to cry, first a little, but before she knew it, she was sobbing into Lisa's shoulder. Someone wrapped a blanket around her.

"Don't worry, Izzie. You're safe now. You're safe."

Izzie looked up just in time to see a helicopter emerge from behind the warehouse and fly off toward the mountains.

TWENTY

They took Aunt Claire away in an ambulance. Isabel sat on a rock near the trees.

She kept trying to ask about Maya, but no one seemed to know anything about her. Isabel feared the worst, as she had all along.

The guilt overwhelmed her.

I wish it had been me. She thought of all that Maya had accomplished and could have accomplished still. She thought of how proud her parents would have been of Maya. She was remarkable.

An officer approached her and asked Isabel to follow her. They walked toward an ambulance parked outside the main building lobby.

"I don't need medical attention," she explained for what felt like the twentieth time. "I'm just a little bruised up."

The officer didn't answer. As they rounded the corner, Isabel saw that the gurney was occupied.

Her eyes met Maya's.

Isabel ran to her sister, sobbing. Maya wrapped her

arms around her and held on tight. They stayed that way a long time before Isabel pulled back.

"Maya, I thought... are you okay? You're hurt?"

"I made it out of the fire, but I did get a pretty big burn, and I think I broke my leg in the process. I tried to help you guys..." Maya started to cry again. "I tried to get to you, but I couldn't walk. I had to hide. I'm sorry, Izzie. I'm so sorry I couldn't help you."

"You did help us, Maya. You saved all of us." The sisters held each other and cried together for a long time.

Lisa walked up. "I'll ride with you girls to the hospital. Claire is there, and she's awake. The police want to talk to you when we get there."

The medics wheeled Maya's gurney into the ambulance. Isabel climbed in after her and Lisa.

The door closed and they began the drive away from Gennovations. Finally.

"What about the animals?" Isabel asked.

"Don't worry about them," Lisa said. "I've asked animal control to round them up and bring them all to the clinic. We will take care of them."

"Even the glow-in-the-dark snake?"

Lisa looked confused.

"Um, yes, I guess so."

"There is a big, overly muscular dog, too. I don't know if he made it. He saved me from Bruce. I hope he's okay."

Lisa put her arm around Isabel.

"How did you get here, Lisa," Maya asked. "What happened?"

"After you girls left my house, I got so worried. I was trying to protect my family, but I knew you were in trouble. I fretted for a few hours and then decided I needed to go to the police. When I got there, I realized how bad things were. Someone had broken in. The dispatcher was out cold, and the phones were ringing. The only officer I could find was injured, but he told me they'd taken you."

She paused for a moment and took a deep breath. "I should never have let you leave my house. I should have gone with you to the police. I should have gone to the police myself."

"It's okay. We understand," Maya said, patting her on the knee.

"Anyway, once I realized how bad this was, I tried to help. I drove out here with the officer from the station, and when we realized we couldn't get in, I called my dad. He's a lawyer, and he has some judge friends. It took forever, but we finally got someone to sign a warrant to let us in."

"And you brought Freddie and Nolan?" Isabel asked.

"I figured if anyone could find you quickly, those two would."

"Do you think Dr. Rodriguez got the data? Do you think they have Aunt Claire's research?" Maya asked.

"I'm sure they don't," said Isabel. "I made a friend, and I am certain he kept the encoding on everything they had."

"I am just so glad you girls are okay," said Lisa.

Maya gasped. "What about Andrew and Sara?"

"They're fine," Isabel and Lisa said simultaneously.

"They were with me 'til the end," said Isabel. "They're good friends."

"They are also on their way to the hospital, just to be checked. Andrew needs a few stitches. You'll see them when we get there."

Isabel took a deep breath and leaned back against the ambulance. She closed her eyes and felt her shoulders relax.

They were together, and they were safe. *Mom and Dad would be proud,* she thought.

She held her sister's hand as they made the long drive back through town and to the hospital.

TWENTY-ONE

Aunt Claire and Maya were put into the same hospital room. Isabel sat in a chair between them. Doctors and nurses came in and out to check on them, and both were taken away for x-rays.

Isabel sat in the room alone, counting her blessings, when Sara knocked gently on the door frame.

"Hey," Isabel said. She stood up and wrapped her in a big hug. "I don't even know what to say. I can't thank you and Andrew enough for sticking with us through all this. I am so sorry I got you involved."

"I'm not. I'm glad we were there, and I'm even more glad we saved all that research. I think your Aunt Claire is going to change the world."

"Me, too. Is Andrew okay?"

"He's a little beat up, but he's okay. He says researchers and security guards don't hit nearly as hard as water polo players."

Isabel chuckled and nodded her head. "Jocks are so weird."

Sara reached out and took Isabel's hands. She looked

her in the eyes and smiled. They stayed that way for a long moment. Isabel's heart pounded hard in her chest.

A knock on the door interrupted them. Andrew stood with his parents.

"You are one tough cookie," he said to Isabel, then put his arms around both girls. "Both of you were pretty amazing in there."

Isabel was disappointed that her moment with Sara was interrupted, but she figured she'd have another one soon.

———

MAYA AND AUNT Claire both needed to spend the night in the hospital. The nurses set up a cot for Isabel. A police officer was stationed outside the door in case Dr. Rodriguez turned up. He hadn't been located at Gennovations.

Aunt Claire had a concussion. Maya did, in fact, have a broken leg, but the doctors were more concerned about her burn. They gave Aunt Claire specific instructions on how to prevent infection for the burn once they took Maya home. The doctors emphasized repeatedly that Maya was to rest. She had a follow up appointment in a few days.

When they got home the next evening and switched on the light, Daisy stared back at them, with an entire rug hanging out of her mouth. The house was completely destroyed. It looked like she had taken a bite out of every conceivable surface. Despite the damage, this made Aunt Claire burst into hysterical laughter. Maya and Isabel followed suit, and within seconds, the three of them were in complete hysterics, standing at the front door.

The cockatoos squawked like crazy from their perch, walking back and forth and stretching out their beautiful feathers. The sounds of the animals and laughter filled Isabel with relief.

When they finally calmed down, Isabel got to work clearing a path that Maya could get through on her crutches. She got her sister something to drink so she could take a pain pill and get some sleep.

Aunt Claire and Isabel helped Maya into her room and into bed. Aunt Claire turned off the light and they walked out.

"You know I should be furious with you, right? You should never have come after me. It was way too dangerous."

"The police couldn't help you. What choice did we have?"

"I hear you hacked the entire Gennovations security system."

Isabel smiled mischievously.

"I don't know whether to be proud or terrified."

"Be proud. Thanks to that and a helpful fellow computer nerd, they never got to your research."

"But how do I get to it again?"

"I backed it up, but those files were on my laptop. I didn't feel safe enough to put them on the cloud. I'll try though, Aunt Claire."

Aunt Claire wrapped her into a tight hug and smoothed her hair.

"You're really something."

Isabel felt like she could stay that way forever.

A FEW DAYS LATER, they were all back at the police station again, giving their statements.

Dr. Rodriguez was still missing. The police were very worried he might come after them again, so officers were still sitting outside their home day and night, despite Aunt Claire's protests.

When it was Isabel's turn to give her statement, she walked into the conference room, sat in the chair, and pulled a small flash drive from her pocket. She slid it across the table to Officer Williams, who was sitting with several prosecutors.

"There's my statement."

"What's this?" a woman in a suit asked.

"I think you've all heard that I hacked into their security system." They all exchanged looks with each other. "Well, I recorded the whole thing."

"I thought your computer was destroyed."

"It was, but I had this uploading directly to a file-sharing network, just in case I didn't get out."

"This is... video? Video of the whole thing?"

Isabel sat back in her chair and smiled. "Video of the whole thing."

The group looked at her with wide eyes. Isabel knew they were thrilled. Then one of them picked up the jump drive and walked toward the door.

"Go ahead," she told them. "Watch it."

It, of course, would take hours to watch, so Isabel gave them a general statement of what happened. She offered to provide additional details later if they needed them.

"BE A GOOD BOY, BRUISER," Isabel said, scratching her new friend behind the ears. The big dog from Gennovations that had saved her from Bruce had made it out of the facility with just a broken leg. Aunt Claire has been very attentive to him and patched him up. He took to her the same way he had taken to Isabel. It made Isabel sad to think he'd probably never had any love or affection, which was why he was so sweet when he got it from them. He also really seemed to get along with Freddie, so he'd recently come to live with them. "We will be back after the game."

Maya crutched her way into the room, looking dejected.

"I'm sorry you don't get to play tonight," said Aunt Claire, coming up behind her. "I know it must be killing you."

Maya didn't say anything. She just crutched her way to the door and awkwardly through the frame.

The car ride was quiet. Isabel could tell Maya was nervous for her team. She and Aunt Claire didn't know how best to be supportive—tell her they'd win without her or tell her they wouldn't?

When they arrived at the school, Andrew and Sara were waiting outside with their parents. Sara ran up to greet them.

"We were hoping we could sit with you," she said.

"Of course." Aunt Claire said from behind her. "That would be great."

When they walked into the gymnasium, Isabel could not believe her eyes. People were seated already and when Maya walked in, they all began to cheer. They gave her a standing ovation. Several people held large signs that said things like "MVP Maya" and "Maya saves the day... again!"

Isabel looked on in awe before turning to her sister. Maya was crying and slowly gazing around the room. Behind her, Andrew and Sara beamed and clapped loudly, as did Aunt Claire and their parents.

Isabel stepped closer to Sara. "Did you guys do this?"

Sara smiled bigger and shrugged her shoulders.

When the crowd finally settled down, Maya moved toward the seats.

"No, Maya!" yelled one of the volleyball players. "Over here."

They had cleared a seat on the bench for her. Maya crutched over to her team. One by one, they stood up and hugged her. Maya couldn't stop crying. Her coach wrapped her in a huge bear hug and started to cry, too.

The rest of them went to sit on the bleachers. For the first time ever, Isabel got really into the game. She cheered for the team as they scored and groaned when they didn't. She was on the edge of her seat for the last game. It was tied up, and they had to win to be State champions.

Isabel looked over at Maya. She was standing up now, leaning on her crutches and yelling.

Maya's team scored. One more point to go for the win.

Isabel held her breath. Sara reached over and held her hand.

A tall girl served the ball, and it volleyed back and forth several times before Maya's team set up a perfect spike and shot the ball over. The other team dove but missed. They'd won.

The crowd, including Isabel, went completely wild. The team was in a big group hug down on the court, Maya right in the center.

Aunt Claire reached over and squeezed Isabel. "She needed that."

"Actually, I think I did, too," Isabel replied.

TWENTY-TWO

Maya got out of going to school because of her injury, but Isabel was back by Thursday. She was eager to get to programming so she could dive in. She hoped she could retrieve Aunt Claire's research, but she wasn't optimistic.

As she walked through the hallways, she heard a group of girls sneer behind her. She turned to see Jessica and her friends staring at her.

"What's your problem?" she demanded, marching up to Jessica, who stood tall. She wore a look of superiority on her overly made-up face.

"Oh nothing. Just wondering if you are living amongst the animals now. Is your aunt doing experiments on you, too? Is that why you're so weird?"

Isabel smiled sweetly.

"Hey Jessica, if you think sharing a picture of your awkward phase is the worst thing I could do to you, you are very sadly mistaken."

Jessica's smile dropped.

"Any idea how easy it is for me to hack a social media

account? Or even your texts? Or... wait for it... your home's security system."

"You couldn't do any of that. That's illegal."

Isabel laughed in her face.

She pulled out her phone, typed in a simple command, and waited. All the phones nearby started to beep. A girl showed Jessica her screen. The girl had received a text from Jessica that said, "Try me."

Jessica looked horrified.

"I... I... " she shook her head side to side.

"Leave me alone, Jessica. And leave Sara Banks alone, too."

Jessica nodded quickly.

Isabel headed to class. Now she was running late. Sara ran up alongside her.

"That was amazing. How did you even do that?"

"Oh, I hacked her phone a long time ago. I thought it might be useful one day."

Sara laughed.

"I've got to go." Isabel ducked into the classroom, waving at Sara behind her.

Inside the classroom, Isabel got comfortable in her usual spot in the back of the room. Mr. Marcks told the class what to work on, then asked Isabel to step out into the hallway.

"I heard a little bit about what went on over the weekend."

Isabel nodded.

"I understand you were able to hack into a pretty high-tech security system, and you encoded a great deal of data."

"Yeah, all true."

Mr. Marcks exhaled and ran his fingers through his hair.

"You should probably be teaching this class."

Isabel laughed. "I would rather not. I don't want everyone to know my secrets."

Mr. Marcks smiled at her.

"I am trying now to track down some data that was housed on a destroyed hard drive. I think it's a lost cause, but it's important so I'm going to keep trying," Isabel told him, confiding in him about her work for the first time. "That's why I am sitting in the back and not paying any attention to your assignment. Sorry, but maybe this could be a special project or something?" She smiled and folded her hands in front of her.

"Hmm. I think I actually might be able to help with that."

"Really?"

"I can't do anything about it myself, but I have a friend who is a real whiz. I'll try to get ahold of him for you."

"Thanks, Mr. Marcks."

The next day, Isabel walked into the classroom to find Greg sitting in her normal spot.

"Greg!" Isabel exclaimed. "What are you doing here?"

"I'm a friend of Mr. Marcks. He called me and said he had a student who could use my help. I had a feeling I knew who it might be."

Isabel beamed.

"Although, considering how good you are, I don't know if I will be much help to you. What are we working on?"

Isabel was filled with hope.

For the next few days, Greg came into the classroom every day to help Isabel. His inside knowledge of the Gennovations systems helped Isabel to start accessing the systems she wanted.

"What's going on at Gennovations now, anyways?" she asked one day.

"The place is swarming with lawyers," Greg said. "Now that Dr. Rodriguez is gone, they're trying to distance themselves from him and just manage the liability of the facility. I don't know if they really knew everything he was up to. They thought he was the leading researcher on this stuff. No one knew his plans."

"The security team did."

"He had them convinced he was doing lifesaving work and Claire was the one creating problems, at least that's what they are claiming now. It turns out 'Steve Rodriguez' wasn't even his real name."

Isabel rolled her eyes.

"We are all getting fired though," he added. "They offered us severance checks and asked us to make Friday our last day. I'm thrilled about it."

"I bet."

They continued their work each afternoon. At every breakthrough, they would high five or cheer, and the rest of the class would turn around and give them very confused looks—especially the day when they finally got what they wanted and literally broke into a dance in the back of the room, right in the middle of Mr. Marcks lesson.

"You have the same victory dance as your sister," laughed Tavi from the front of the classroom.

THAT NIGHT, they ate dinner at home, Chinese takeout, sitting around their table. Isabel was so excited she was having trouble sitting still. When she couldn't take it anymore, she blurted out, "I have a present for you!"

Aunt Claire looked up mid-bite. She raised her eyebrows and smiled.

Isabel pulled a small box out of her pocket. It was wrapped with a bow on it, though the bow was sort of crushed from being in her pocket.

Isabel beamed and wiggled around as Aunt Claire opened it. She took the lid off the box, and inside was a tiny flash drive.

Aunt Claire's face grew very serious. She picked up the drive and held it up.

"Is this what I think it is, Izzie?"

An enormous smile grew across Maya's face as she realized what was happening.

"Down to every last piece of scratch paper. Everything digitized, and all of the encoding removed."

Aunt Claire screamed and jumped out of her chair, sending Lo Mein flying. Freddie bounded to the spilled food while everyone was distracted. The cockatoos yelled "IZZIE! IZZIE! IZZIE!"

Aunt Claire was dancing around the dining room. Bruiser came in and wagged his tail. It was the most beautiful chaos Isabel had ever seen. This must be what it feels like to score the winning point in a game. She turned to look at Maya, and they high fived.

ACKNOWLEDGMENTS

Bill, none of it happens without you. None of it. I write a lot of words, but I'll never have the words to express how much your support means to me. Thank you.

Thank you to my family for all of their support of this and a million other projects. Thank you, Mom, for being my biggest cheerleader. For as long as I can remember, you've never missed an opportunity to cheer me on. Thank you, Dad, for giving me the right foundation for success. Thank you, Tyler, for your excitement over this book despite it not being sports. Thank to Kelly and Max for your support and for giving me the world's most wonderful reading buddy.

To Marie and Judy—my work would never be what it is without your ideas and inspiration. I love reading your books and can't wait to see them published.

Thank you to my first agent, Kristina Slater for taking a chance on me, and to my agent, Stephanie Hanson, for sticking with me. Thank you, Amy Brewer, for helping to make this series a reality. Thank you, Jodi Thompson and TwylaBeth Lambert, for loving this story enough to bring it to the world and working so hard to make it even better.

Thanks to all my friends for your encouragement, celebrations, and early fandom of this series.

Thank you to every reader, teacher, librarian, and parent who puts books in the hands of kids and helps them explore through their imaginations. And thank you, reader, for spending some time with Isabel, Maya, Aunt Claire, and all their friends.

If you enjoyed this book and would like more, please have an adult help you do one or more of the following:

- Leave a review on your favorite book review site
- Tell a friend about *Aunt Claire's Pet Care* and Katie Evans
- Ask your local library to put Katie Evans's work on the shelf
- Recommend Fawkes Press books to your local bookstore

Visit us online
www.AuthorKatieEvans.com
www.FawkesPress.com

FAWKES PRESS

COMING SOON!